BEDBUGS

BEDBUGS

Ben H. Winters

QUIRK BOOKS
PHILADELPHIA

Library of Congress Cataloging in Publication Number: 2011922691

ISBN: 978-1-59474-523-2

Printed in Canada

Typeset in Bembo

Designed by Doogie Horner
Cover photo by Jonathan Pushnik
Production management by John J. McGurk

Quirk Books
215 Church Street
Philadelphia, PA 19106
quirkbooks.com

10 9 8 7 6 5 4 3 2 1

FOR DI

BOOK I

1.

"Hey, Al. Come look at this one."

Susan Wendt studied the screen of her MacBook while her husband, Alex, paused the DVR and walked over to the kitchen table. He read the Craigslist ad over her shoulder and delivered a quick verdict: "Bull crap." He cracked his knuckles and scootched behind her to get to the fridge. "It's total bull crap, baby."

"Hmm. Maybe."

"Gotta be. You want?"

He held up a Brooklyn Lager by the neck and waggled it back and forth. Susan shook her head, scanning the Craigslist ad with a slight frown. Alex opened the beer and went to crouch beside her. "It's one of those where the broker lures you in and then goes, 'Oh *that* place? That place got taken *yesterday!* How about this one? Rent is *joost* a *leeeeedle beeeet* more expensive....'" He slipped into a goofy gloss on the thick Brazilian accent of the most recent broker to take them on a wild-goose chase through half of south Brooklyn. Susan laughed.

"But wait," she said, pointing at the screen again. "It's not a broker. See? 'For rent by owner.'"

Alex raised his eyebrows skeptically, took a swallow of the beer, and wandered back to the TV.

Their apartment search, now two and a half months old, had been her thing more than his all along. He felt that their current place, a one-bedroom-plus-office-nook off Union Square, was perfect. Or, if not perfect, then at least perfectly fine. And the idea of moving, the logistics and the packing and the various expenditures—it all made him want to tear his own head off. Or so he rather vividly expressed it.

"Plus," Alex had argued, "I'm not sure this is the time to jack up our rent."

Susan had been calm but insistent: it *was* time. It was time for Emma to have a proper bedroom, one that wasn't a converted office nook; time for Susan to have a place to set up her easel and paints; time for Alex to have a real kitchen to cook his elaborate meals. "And rents are a heck of a lot lower than they used to be, especially in Brooklyn. Besides, Alex," she had concluded, making a blatant appeal to his vanity, "you're doing really well right now. Come on. We can just look, right?"

Alex had relented, and "just looking" rapidly escalated into a full-on search. Every evening that summer, after Emma had her bath and went to bed, while Alex settled in for his nightly dose of god-awful reality television, Susan trolled Craigslist and Rentals.com and the *Times* real estate section, entering rents and square footage and broker's phone numbers on a master spreadsheet dotted with hyperlinks. On the weekends the family tromped from open house to open house, from Fort Greene to Boerum Hill, clutching cups of deli coffee and informational folders from Corcoran, pushing Emma in her bright-pink Maclaren stroller.

They'd found places they loved for way too much, places in their price range that they hated, and, for occasional variety, places they couldn't afford and hated anyway. Last weekend they'd schlepped all the way to Red Hook, riding the F train to Smith and Ninth and then the B61 the rest of the way. The apartment they'd seen there, a converted artists' loft on Van Brunt Street, was Susan's favorite so far. It was footsteps from Fairway, cater-corner from a hipster bakery famous for its salted-caramel tarts, and featured a master bedroom with a thin slice of East River view.

But the apartment was forty-five minutes from the city, and with no utilities included it was just north of their budget.

"We really can't push it on price," Alex said, shaking his head. "Especially with you not working right now."

Susan had smiled tightly, hiding her deep disappointment at his veto. She'd been increasingly and painfully aware, as the apartment search continued, that she had little leverage on the question of cost. It was true—she *wasn't* working just then, a state of affairs Alex had totally supported, but it didn't give her a lot of leeway on rent. She carefully transcribed the details of the "for rent by owner" Craigslist ad into the spreadsheet on her MacBook. They hadn't even *looked* in Brooklyn Heights, because—well, what the hell for? No one was renting two-bedrooms in the Heights for under four thousand dollars a month, recession or not. No one except (Susan copied the name carefully from the ad) Andrea Scharfstein, who was offering the top two floors of her Cranberry Street brownstone: "1300 sq. ft., 2BR 2B, d/w, ample closets." All for a startling $3,550.

"Thirty-five-fifty?" Alex snorted, fast-forwarding through a commercial break. "Bull crap, baby. Guaranteed."

*

When Alex, Susan, and Emma arrived on Cranberry Street a little before their scheduled appointment at 10:30 the next morning,

Andrea Scharfstein was waiting for them on the top step of her front stoop, reading the Sunday *New York Times* and sipping tea from a big yellow mug with the WNYC logo blazoned on the side. As they approached, their pink stroller bouncing over the uneven slate of the sidewalk, Andrea folded the newspaper and stood squinting down at them with her hands on hips: a thin and frail old woman with a big cloud of curly steel-gray hair, wearing a sixties-fabulous peach sundress, a gauzy taupe shawl, and big chunky bracelets on both wrists.

"Look at this! Right on time," she said approvingly, glancing down at her watch. Susan unbuckled Emma and scooped her out so Alex could fold the Maclaren. "I like you people already."

"Hi!" called Emma, climbing the tall steps with an exaggerated, marching stride, clinging to the banister. "I'm Emma."

"Of course you are, dear! And a lovelier specimen of Emma I've never seen. Did you pick your name?"

"No!" Emma giggled. "My mama and dada picked it."

"Good for them. My name is Andrea."

Alex followed Emma, steadying her with a hand at the small of her back, while Susan lingered at the bottom, taking in the facade. The house at 56 Cranberry Street had steep concrete front steps, ascending from a little black wrought-iron gate to the oversized front door, which was painted in a rich and pleasing orangey red. Surrounding the stoop was a front garden, overgrown with azaleas, crab grass, and small flowering trees. The house itself was red brick, with wooden shutters framing neat lines of windows, three per floor. There were window boxes, growing what looked like herbs, in the windows of the first-floor apartment—Andrea's apartment.

I bet it has pressed-tin ceilings, thought Susan, and then—suddenly, fiercely—*I really want to live here.* She teased herself as she caught up with Emma and Alex at the top of the steps.

Down, girl. You wanna see the inside first?

"You folks move quickly, I'll give you that," said Andrea Scharfstein, shaking their hands briskly. "You called maybe five minutes after I wrote that ad. Or what am I supposed to say? After I 'posted' it. Anyway, ten minutes, at the most." Andrea's hand in Susan's was dry and papery. She spoke quickly, with a voice that was thin and the slightest bit gravelly, like she was on the verge of a cough. Beneath the bushy mass of hair, her face was a map of small lines and spots—from her face and body, which was slight and stooped, Susan would have put Andrea at seventy or older. But there was a sharpness and snap about her movements, a vigor that defied her physical appearance.

"Well, follow me, this way, here we go," Andrea said briskly, turning the handle of the big front door and leaning into it with a thin shoulder. Susan was fleetingly and pleasantly reminded of Willy Wonka leading the wide-eyed contest winners into his chocolate factory for the first time. "Grab that mug for me, Alex. Is it Alex? It is, yes? If I leave a mug out here with even a drop of tea in it, we'll have ants in no time."

Emma trotted fearlessly inside, a step ahead of Andrea, looking around in the dimly lit downstairs landing. "Is this your house?" she asked.

"It is," answered Andrea, patting the girl on the head. "What do you think?"

"It's really good."

Andrea took Emma's hand and helped her up the interior stairs to the second-floor landing. *I want to live here,* Susan thought again, almost defiantly, and this time she didn't bother to chastise herself.

Instead she glanced at Alex, who had paused beneath the one dusty light fixture, a cheap chandelier shedding haphazard illumination on the stairwell. Susan felt like she could read his mind—he was cataloging flaws, looking for reasons to reject this charming and quaint old house. *The stone of the stoop is slightly crumbling; the paint on the door is chipped and fading.*

Susan didn't care. This was where she wanted to live.

*

The interior stairway led one flight up and ended at a small carpeted landing with a single door.

"It doesn't say 'number two' on the door," said Andrea. "I hope that doesn't bother you. You'd have to be pretty stupid not to find your own apartment. You just come in, come up the stairs." Susan laughed politely, and Andrea smiled gently at her. "It was one big house, of course, until I lost my husband, Howard. I suppose it's possible I'm still resistant to the change."

As Andrea cleared her throat noisily and led them inside, Susan wondered how long ago that change had occurred; how many other tenants had there been? There was something about Andrea that suggested the sturdy, independent spirit of a longtime widow. Following her bent back down the long front hallway of the apartment, Susan felt a wave of sympathy for this woman, smart and lively as she was, growing old and dying here alone.

The door opened onto a hallway that ran lengthwise down the entire apartment, and featured not one but two coat closets. The expansive hallway ended, on the Cranberry Street side, in a bright and cozy kitchen, with granite countertops and a decent, if not overwhelming, amount of pantry space. "So the kitchen's not eat-in?" asked Alex, and shot a significant look over Andrea's head, which Susan could easily translate: *not a lot of space for cooking. . . .*

Susan just smiled. The kitchen in their current apartment was so small, the refrigerator and oven couldn't be used at the same time, because the doors banged into each other. She ran her fingers along the countertops and crouched to open and close the cupboards while Emma played don't-step-on-the-crack on the hardwood floor. Above the stove a pair of windows faced onto Cranberry Street, filling the room with gorgeous midmorning sunlight that cast the floorboards in lustrous browns.

"Floor's maybe a little uneven," Alex noted, crouching to run his palms disapprovingly along the ground.

Andrea shrugged. "Yes, yes. Actually, Howard was meaning to redo the floors in the whole place, but somehow we never had time." Alex nodded as he straightened. Susan glanced down; the floors looked A-OK to her.

"This building was first constructed in 1864, the same year as the Brooklyn Bridge. But it's a solid old thing, and it's got plenty of character. Much like myself." She gave Alex a broad, almost vaudevillian wink, then brayed throaty laughter. Alex smiled politely and gave Susan another meaningful glance: *We're sure we want this old loon as a landlord?* But Susan ignored him and laughed along with Andrea. Emma, too, squealed and hid her mouth behind her hands—at three and a half years old, she loved jokes, even when she had no idea what they were about.

"Oh, by the way, in case you happen to care, the ceiling?" Andrea gestured upward with a thumb. "That's pressed tin."

2.

If Susan had any doubts about the apartment, the thing that sold her on it, absolutely and irrevocably—what made her certain in the core of her being that she *had* to live at 56 Cranberry Street #2—was the bonus room.

At the opposite end of the apartment's first floor from the kitchen, back down the long entrance hallway and through an arch framed by two funky old-fashioned sconces, was the living room, spacious and irregularly rectangular, with light flooding in from two big back windows. The center of the far wall bulged into the room like a semicircular column; it was an odd architectural detail, and at first Susan thought there might be a pillar behind it. Closer inspection revealed it to be an air shaft, separating 56 Cranberry Street from the house next door. It even had two decent-size windows, which let in yet more light.

"Very strange, I know," said Andrea of the shaft, tapping on one of its windows with a big costume-jewelry gold ring she wore on her pinky. "It runs from the roof all the way down to the basement. You'll see when we go upstairs, it cuts through the bathroom up there. Lots of light, though, lets in lots of light."

"Cool," said Susan, and Alex peered through one of the windows, craning his neck to look up and down the shaft.

"My best guess is, it was a dumbwaiter when this house was first built," Andrea continued. "Run drinks from the kitchen up to the second floor, that sort of thing. One time a bird got in there somehow and couldn't get out. Flapped around and made the most pitiful noises until it died. Awful. Just awful."

Even Alex couldn't criticize the living room, considering their current apartment didn't even *have* one. While Andrea stood with hands on hips in the archway and Emma walked the room's periphery, playing some complicated game of counting steps, Susan slipped next to him and squeezed his hand.

"What are you thinking?" she whispered.

Before he could respond, Andrea strode across the room and pulled open a door in the left rear corner—a small door, painted the same color as the wall, so innocuous that Susan hadn't even realized it was there.

"Back here is this funny little room," she said, gesturing them over for a look. "I call it the bonus room, because it's sort of, you know, a bit of something extra. It's what we would have called the 'sewing room,' when I was a child. Of course, when I was a child we were sewing sweaters for our pet dinosaurs."

"Pet dinosaurs!" Emma shrieked, raising her hands to her mouth in exaggerated amazement. *"Whaaaat?!"*

"This one, I like," said Andrea, patting Emma on the head while Alex smiled.

Susan stepped into the bonus room. It was barely a room at all, really, more of an overgrown closet, with the one door and a single window, letting in a steady and unbroken stream of golden light.

This is it, Susan thought, experiencing such a powerful wave of joy that she had to clamp her hands to her mouth to keep from whooping aloud. *This is it!*

She'd had second thoughts galore since leaving her job last year. Second thoughts, third thoughts, and more—it seemed so audacious, so unrealistic, so selfish, after all this time to abandon her career and "go back to her painting." But she had done it. She had worked up the nerve to tell Alex what she was considering and found him to be not only understanding, but incredibly supportive: "Of course," he'd said. "If that's what you want, we'll make it work." She'd given her notice and gone to Sam's to supply herself with new brushes, new oils and pastels and turpentine. And then . . . somehow, the subsequent months had flown by, and Susan found one reason after another to put off starting. She'd gotten involved in a friend's run for city council, spent a month going door to door with pamphlets, collecting signatures; Emma had been seriously ill for five days, ended up at New York-Presbyterian one harrowing night with an IV line; they'd gone to Alex's parents for a week in July; and then of course she'd decided their apartment was too small, and they had to move.

Things kept interfering—or, as Susan knew very well, she *let* things keep interfering, so that she wouldn't have to face this enormous life change she'd set up for herself. But now, in this room . . .

When she was at Legal Aid, counting the hours until she could go home, feeling like a fraud and a liar, her toes throbbing in her pinchy black work shoes, she would indulge flights of fancy in which she stood painting on a sunny midmorning, bathed in a shaft of sunlight and lost in a cloud of artistic effort. On such occasions it was just this kind of room in which she always imagined herself.

God, Susan thought, tears welling in her eyes. *I don't even think it was this* kind *of room. It was this exact room.*

"I didn't even mention it in the ad," said Andrea, as she and Alex

ducked into the room and stood next to Susan. "I'd feel like a huck-
ster, because you can hardly count it as a room. Good for storage,
though. Or a nursery."

"Or a studio," Susan said softly.

"Oh? Are you an artist?"

"Well, it's kind of a long story. I was—I mean, I am. But—"

"Yes," interrupted Alex, throwing his arm over her shoulder.
"She is."

*

Emma was getting antsy, so Susan set her up in the center of the
empty living room, producing from her oversized pocketbook a box
of crayons, a stack of construction paper, and a small snack of dried
fruit and cheese.

"Stay in this room, please," said Alex, and Emma nodded without looking up, already deeply engaged in her coloring.

"My goodness, she's a happy duck, isn't she?" said Andrea as she
led Susan and Alex up the narrow uncarpeted staircase to the second
floor. "Howard and I never had any of our own, but I've always loved
children. Even the miserable snot-nose types, but especially happy
little ducks like yours."

The second floor was really just two large rooms, a master bedroom and a second bedroom, separated by the staircase landing and
a decent linen closet. The upstairs bathroom, where the air shaft
ended in a small arced skylight, was large, with room for both a
shower stall and a full jetted tub. At the sight of it, Alex whispered a
mock-lascivious "hey now" into Susan's neck, and she nudged him
playfully. The master bedroom, like the kitchen downstairs, faced

Cranberry Street and was similarly bathed in warm and generous light.

"All these windows are double paned, by the by," said Andrea, rapping on the sturdy glass. "Noise reducing. Work like the devil. I got 'em downstairs in my apartment, too."

*

On the way out, Susan asked to see the bonus room one more time. While Alex spoke to Andrea in his low, all-business voice, she walked in a slow, enchanted circle around the tiny room and then stopped to rest her hands on the windowsill and gaze outside. The small back lot was separated from the mirror-image lot, belonging to a house on Orange Street, by a weathered wooden fence. The lot was overgrown with wild grass and dotted with bent and spindly trees; Susan wondered which of these gnarled beauties she would paint first.

From all the way down the hall she heard Andrea's voice saying, "So I'm sorry about that . . . " and then something she couldn't hear, to which Alex replied, ". . . I know how it is . . ." Then Andrea laughed a dry rustling titter and said, "Well, the less said about them, the better." Emma could be heard giggling and hooting, having coronated herself princess of the living room, with a host of invisible subjects.

Turning from the window, Susan was suddenly struck by a sour unsavory odor, a nasty staleness in the closed air of the room. She crinkled her nose, and in the next breath it was gone.

She shut the door of the bonus room behind her, gathered up her daughter, and found Andrea and Alex in the kitchen, framed by the slanting sunlight. Andrea was nodding vigorously, eyes narrowed with interest, leaning into the conversation.

"A photographer?" she said. "Is that a fact?

"It is," Alex said.

"Two artists! My humble abode will be quite the atelier."

Susan glanced uneasily at her husband. Alex was not an art photographer—not anymore. Like Susan, he had begun his postcollege life
a decade ago with high artistic aspirations. Unlike Susan, who had
folded up her easel after eighteen months of desultory effort and gone
to law school as her parents had always intended, Alex had bopped
along for a while, enjoying just enough success to encourage him but
never enough to make a living. What he had found instead was an unusual niche in the world of commercial photography, at which he had
been unexpectedly successful—so successful, in fact, that he hadn't
taken what he would consider a "real" photograph in years.

"I'm not really an artist," Alex told Andrea. His tone was light,
unoffended, and Susan exhaled. "I own a small company called Gem-
Flex. We take pictures of diamonds and other precious stones, for
jewelry catalogs and advertisements."

"Really? How interesting!"

"Ah. That's where you're wrong," said Alex, giving Andrea an
easy lopsided grin. "But it pays the bills."

Back outside on the stoop, they all shook hands. Andrea knelt
with some effort to give Emma a hug, which the girl surprisingly
accepted.

"Thank you so much for showing the apartment to us," said
Susan. "We'll be in touch soon, OK?"

"Take your time, take your time," said Andrea, and coughed. "But
I've got a good feeling about you people. I do."

They had Emma all buckled in when Alex turned back and
called, "Oh, hey, Andrea? One more thing."

Susan squeezed her eyes shut: *here we go.* He was fishing for a problem, for a reason to exercise his magical with-you-not-working-right-now veto, to keep them entombed in their one-bedroom on Twelfth Street for all eternity. *The place is amazing, Alex,* she thought. *This is where we're going to live. Just accept it.*

"You seem like you'd be a great landlord," he was saying. "But if there are, I don't know, problems, with the heat or the toilet or whatever—"

Andrea interrupted with her high, throaty, barking laugh.

"Oh, good heavens! *No.* These ancient hands will not be plunging your toilet." She held up thin, knotty fingers. "There's a nice gentleman, an old friend, who is very handy and takes care of all that sort of thing for me. He can handle anything. I promise."

"Oh," said Alex, seeming mollified. "Well, great, then."

That's my girl, thought Susan, and beamed up at Andrea, who waved.

"All right, folks. See you soon."

*

It was three or four blocks down Cranberry Street to the Brooklyn Heights Promenade, where Emma hopped out of the stroller for some much-needed running around. Susan and Alex leaned on the railing and stood side by side, gazing out across the broad expanse of the East River at the Statue of Liberty, the Chrysler Building, and the skyline hole where the World Trade Center had once stood. Susan glanced furtively at her husband over the top of her Ray-Bans, trying to assess his state of mind. It was turning into a hot day, and she wore not only her sunglasses but a big floppy hat to protect herself from the sun. She had sensitive blue eyes and the kind of pale Scandinavian skin that burned easily; Alex, rugged and dark, had no such problems. He never bothered to wear sunscreen, which made Susan envious and, occasionally, mildly irritated.

They turned their backs to the railing and saw Emma streak by, shrieking merrily, in fervid pursuit of an adorable little boy in blue Crocs and a windbreaker, his hair in neat cornrows.

"All right, dear, moment of truth," Susan said at last. "What do you think?"

"Well, I think a lot of things." He let out a long breath and stroked his chin thoughtfully. "Did you hear? Her last tenants ran out on her, so she's asking for three months' security deposit."

"Three months? Jesus." Susan did some quick math in her head. "So that's—"

"It's ridiculous, is what it is."

"Can we afford it?"

"We can, because the rent is crazy low. I mean, really insanely low. In fact—" Alex gave Susan his most serious pretend-serious face. "It's probably haunted, right? Gotta be haunted."

Susan cracked up and rested her head on his shoulder. She had a good feeling about where this conversation was going. "Totally," she said. "Built on the only Indian burial ground in Brooklyn Heights."

"Shame," he said. "Because otherwise it's fabulous."

"It is, right? And a great neighborhood. *And* an easy commute for you."

"Yup."

"And, it's got that . . . what did she call it?" Susan pretended to try and remember. "The bonus room. It'll make a great studio, I think."

"Right. Now, did you notice? No washer/dryer."

"Eh. I'll live."

Susan looked around for Emma and found her right away, on a nearby bench with the little boy, chatting merrily with a woman Susan guessed was the boy's mother. Susan pointed to herself and then to Emma, mouthing "she's mine," and the other woman smiled back and waved cheerily.

God, Susan thought. *I love it here.*

"So, OK," Susan said, turning back to Alex. "Why don't we sleep on it tonight, and . . . " She trailed off and broke into a surprised smile. Alex had his phone out.

"Screw it," he said, grinning. "Let's call her right now."

Susan's heart leaped in her chest.

"Yeah?"

"Yeah. We both know we're going to take it. So let's just take it."

As Alex dialed Andrea Scharfstein, Susan felt a sharp sting on her calf and bent to smack at the mosquito. She nailed it, and her palm came up bearing a thick bloody smear.

*

Andrea sent the lease three hours later to Susan via e-mail, exactly as she had promised. After Emma was asleep and after Alex left for a long-scheduled and eagerly anticipated game of Texas Hold 'Em with some college cronies, Susan sat down to review it.

"I'll take a look when I get home," Alex promised.

"Sure you will," said Susan, and gave him a kiss as he headed out the door.

He would, naturally, be drunk later, or at least buzzed, and the truth was she didn't really need his help. She was, after all, the lawyer. *Well,* Susan thought with a smile, as the document emerged from their sleek miniature laser printer, *former lawyer.*

The lease was obviously cut and pasted from a sample document floating around on the Internet. Across the top margin it said: SAMPLE OF A NEW YORK STATE RENTAL AGREEMENT, MODIFY AS NEEDED. But Andrea had not, so far as Susan could tell, modified it in the slightest. Still, it took her more than an hour to read through everything, not counting ten minutes of comforting Emma, who woke crying from an upsetting dream: in it, she said, while Susan kissed the tears from her cheeks, "Big Grandpa was chasing me"—Alex's grandfather had died seven months ago—"and his face was all melty, like it was big chunks coming off of him." Susan had no idea what could have inspired such an unsettling vision of decomposing, sliding flesh. She got Emma a glass of water and sang "Little Eliza Jane," stroking her soft brown hair until she fell asleep.

Alex got home after midnight, mildly but pleasantly drunk, rambling giddily about the monster pot he'd won by making trip sevens on the river.

"I have no idea what you're talking about. But nice work," said Susan. "You ready to sign a lease?"

He grinned. "Totally." Alex fell into the seat next to her and grabbed the pen. His sleeves were rolled up unevenly, and he smelled like cigars. "Oh! Wait! Shit. There was this guy at Anton's, a lawyer, named Kodaly—Kodiak? Something. Starts with a *K.*"

"Uh-huh?"

"He said the person has to, like, *promise* the place doesn't have bedbugs."

"Well, no. Not exactly." Susan turned the pages of the document and found the clause the mysterious Kodiak was referring to. "Here. 'The landlord or lessor warrants that the premises so leased or rented and all areas used in connection therewith in common with other tenants or residents are fit for human habitation.' Blah, blah, blah, et cetera. It's called a warrant of habitability, and . . . " Susan stopped. "Um, excuse me?"

"What?" Alex asked with sing-song innocence. He had leaned over in his chair toward hers and was busily working his hands into her shirt, fumbling for her breasts. Susan leaned back into his arms.

"I thought you wanted to hear about the bedbugs."

"Not so much, as it turns out."

*

As always, Alex fell asleep almost instantly after sex, sprawled out naked on top of the sheets; Susan lay awake, reading and listening to him breathe softly. After knowing him eight years, and being married for five, she still could not say whether or not she found her husband handsome. Attractive, yes: Alex was tall and solidly constructed, with dark hair and coloring, and he radiated a kind of easy magnetism—especially when he was smiling, which was most of the time. But there was also a kind of roughness about him, a coarseness in his features when you caught them in the wrong light. And the largeness of his body and features, the same largeness that made Susan feel safe and protected when he laughed and threw his arms around her, was a little scary when he was being sullen and aggressive.

Susan pulled on her robe, poked her head into the curtained nook to check on Emma—sleeping soundly now, looking startlingly like her father in her open-mouthed dead-to-the-world repose—

and padded back to the kitchen table and her MacBook. She e-mailed Andrea and said the lease would be on the way back tomorrow with the appropriate checks; she e-mailed their management company to let them know this would be their last month on their month-to-month lease; she went to the website of Moishe's, a moving company she had used in the past, filled out their detailed move-request form, and pressed "submit."

It was now 2:47 a.m. on August 16, 2010. They were traveling to visit Alex's parents on Labor Day weekend, so on the move-request form Susan had indicated they'd like to move to Brooklyn on September 12, a Sunday.

3.

The week after Labor Day, the week preceding their move, the news was dominated by a grisly murder that had occurred in Downtown Brooklyn, just one neighborhood over from the Heights. As was relentlessly reported on 1010 WINS and WCS-880, the twenty-four-hour news stations Susan listened to compulsively—especially when she was at home working on a large project, like packing—a young mother had killed her three-month-old twins. It was an unsettling crime, irresistible to the news stations because of the horrific and strange way the children had been killed; and, as Alex pointed out, because the alleged murderess was young, privileged, and white. The woman, whose name was Anna Mara Phelps, had taken her two daughters in their big black Phil and Ted's double stroller to the roof of their sixteen-story luxury building and then rolled it off the edge, with the infants still inside.

Horror-struck bystanders had watched the giant carriage flipping end over end as it plummeted toward Livingston Street, where it shattered, killing the babies on impact. Phelps was charged with double homicide and considered likely to plead guilty by reason of insanity. On the day of the move, while Alex supervised the crew from Moishe's, Susan took Emma to buy picture hangers at a hardware store on Court and Livingston. She stopped to stare at the spot where the stroller had landed, now marked by a massive shrine of flowers and toys and dolls.

"Well," Alex said sardonically when she described the mournful scene, "welcome to the neighborhood."

*

The movers were done by quarter to five, and Alex dipped into his low, all-business voice to thank each one for his hard work and slip him a twenty. Then Emma, Susan, and Alex wandered around their new home, navigating the monolithic wardrobe boxes, upside-down furniture, and lumpy duffel bags filled with clothing, pillow-cases, and knick-knacks.

"Well, folks, we've got our work cut out for us," said Susan.

"First we get the TV set up, right?" Alex replied, half joking.

"Where's Mr. Boogle?" said Emma.

"We didn't put Mr. Boogle in a box, honey. He's around."

Just before six, Andrea Scharfstein knocked on the door holding a bottle of cheap champagne and an autumnal bouquet in a dispos-able plastic vase.

"You made it!" she growled pleasantly.

"That is so sweet of you," said Susan, and she meant it. The last time she'd been welcomed, when she and Alex moved in together on Union Square, it was with a three-page bulleted list of rules and reg-ulations that had been slid under the door by someone from the management company, even though they were home at the time. Andrea's hair was tied back with a green cotton headband, and she wore a plain blue sheath dress. Susan reflected in passing how pretty she must have been, years ago—and still was, in her old-lady way, with wide deep-set eyes and high cheekbones.

"Hi, Andrea!" piped Emma.

"Hello, young lady."

"Did you bring your pet dinosaur?"

"So clever, this one is! You should be on television, dear heart."

Alex invited Andrea to join them for dinner, but she declined, to Susan's relief.

"Oh, please. Get settled first. Another time." On her way out, Andrea gestured to a thin stack of take-out menus she had left on top of a box, and Susan noticed that her hand trembled just the slightest bit. "Try the vegetarian Chinese place, on Montague. I forget what it's called, but it's good."

*

The vegetarian Chinese place on Montague Street was called the Greens, as it turned out, and it *was* good. They ordered vegetarian moo goo gai pan, miso mushroom soup, and something called General Tso's Soy Protein, which Alex proclaimed "vastly better than it sounds." After dinner they dug up towels and shower stuff, plus enough books and toys for Emma to have a decent playtime before she bustled happily off to bed.

"I don't miss old house at *all*," Emma intoned solemnly as Susan tucked her carefully into her white IKEA bed, which the movers had reassembled before leaving.

"Really, sweets? It's OK if you do."

"Of course it's OK," said Emma, her eyes already drifting shut. "But I *don't*."

The movers had also reassembled the big queen-size bed in the master bedroom, a process that Susan had anxiously overseen. The bed was very possibly her favorite possession, and she had agonized over its purchase for several months for reasons both aesthetic and financial. It was a sleek low-slung modernist beauty with a sturdy slatted frame and a black-oak headboard, sold by Design Within Reach for $2,550 plus tax—a significant chunk of change, even back when she *was* working.

True to form, Alex had protested, mildly, that their old double bed was just fine. "What's wrong with it?"

"Well, I've had it since college, for one thing. Plus we're two people. We need a queen."

"But aren't *doubles* for two people? Two? Double?"

Susan had prevailed, arguing in part that a decent bed would help her sleep. She was a chronic insomniac, unlike Alex, who bragged that he could fall asleep in a muddy ditch or stay sleeping through artillery fire—a gift that had been maddening to Susan during Emma's infancy, when he slumbered peacefully through many a late-night screaming session.

After Emma was down they puttered around for a couple hours, drinking Andrea's champagne from plastic cups and unpacking a few boxes marked UNPACK ME FIRST! Susan found the box of perishables and arranged its contents in the pantry while Alex focused on his treasured kitchen gadgets: the coffee grinder, the rice cooker, the nonstick frying pans, the knife block and full set of Henckels Twin Select cooking knives. Finally he yawned, announced that he was exhausted, and headed upstairs.

"I can't believe we have two floors," he said, pausing midway up the steps and gesturing expansively at all their space, in the manner of a Roman emperor. "Nice work, Sue."

Susan finished her champagne and poured herself another cup, adding new items to her to-do list, until her eyes were drooping shut and she admitted to herself there was nothing else that could realistically be accomplished that night. She went upstairs to the bathroom, unzipped her gold toiletries bag, and fished around until she found the Altoids tin in which she kept her Ambien. She counted the pills, each one a perfect little white oblong: there were twenty-seven ten-milligram tablets left, out of an original stash of fifty, prescribed eighteen months ago with instructions to take half a pill when anxiety made it impossible to asleep. On nights like this one, however, with her mind racing through all the upcoming tasks, Susan gave herself a dispensation. Carefully she split a pill with her fingernail, put one half back in the Altoids tin and placed the other half on her tongue, cupped her hands to collect a scoopful of water from the faucet, and washed it down.

But if the Ambien worked, it didn't work nearly enough. The minute Susan's head hit the pillow, her mind busily began annotating and revising the to-do list, which she could see in her mind's eye as clearly as if it were displayed on the iPhone screen in front of her. Unpacking, of course, was at the top of the list, broken down into several subcategories: Emma's things, her and Alex's things, kitchen things, sheets and towels. Now that they had more space, they would need more furniture, and there was a sublist for that, too: small endtables for the living room, some sort of sideboard for the kitchen.

. . . *and could they afford new furniture? How much had the movers ended up charging? Alex would know the exact figure, but Susan couldn't remember—four thousand? five?—plus that massive security deposit—moves were a money sieve, Alex was right . . .*

Susan's restless mind jumped to the universe of small activities, mundane but crucial, that went with setting up a new household: the making of keys, the filling out of address-change forms, the search for good grocery stores. It was to Susan, of course, that most of these tasks would fall.

. . . since you're not working right now . . . since you're not working right now . . .

She looked at her husband, his thick torso, his face squashed in his pillow, a thin line of drool connecting his lower lip to the collar of his ancient Pearl Jam T-shirt, and wondered just how angry he really was at her, just below, or not even below, the surface, how much resentment he harbored. Alex had artistic ambitions, too, after all, which he had long ago boxed up and stashed away, just as she had. But now she was taking hers back out again, unpacking the dreams of her youth like antique linens from an old chest, while he was stuck shooting pictures of watches and diamond rings, pretending to take pride in it . . . supporting her and their child, her and her dilettante ambitions.

Of course he's resentful, he must be, he . . .

Susan took a deep breath. Alex had never expressed any such feelings to her, of course—everything he had said on the subject was quite to the contrary (*"To tell you the truth, Sue, I think it's a great idea!"*)

But that wasn't good enough for Susan, lying awake in the Brooklyn dark in the middle of the night, surrounded by a shadowy forest of wardrobe boxes and furniture in an unfamiliar room. Surely Alex thought terrible things of her, surely he *seethed* every time he looked at her. Why, otherwise, had the question of more children never been raised between them? Somehow the time to bring it up always seemed wrong. Somehow it always felt like if she *did* bring it up, he would launch into a list of reasons why a bigger family was impossible right now, would slam the door on the question, just as he

had slammed the door shut on the artists' loft with a harbor view in
Red Hook . . .

   . . . *oh, hell, Susan, you don't need that place anymore, you got this*
place, remember?

   This thought, vaguely comforting though it was, led her back along
her twisting maze of anxiety, to yet more things that needed to be done:
find out when recycling goes out, find a nonfilthy Laundromat—no
washer/dryer, remember?—look into preschool programs for Emma
for January—she had secured a slot at a well-regarded place in the Flat-
iron District, but now Susan had wrenched up the family and moved
them here, *for no reason, for no good reason* . . .

   Susan sat up, panting, clutching a hand to her chest. "Shit," she
said to the darkness.

   The bedside clock read 2:34. Susan rose, stepped into the bathroom, and took the other half of the Ambien.

                                        *

   Reluctant to return to bed, Susan turned the other way out of
the bathroom, slipped past the linen closet, and creaked open the
door of Emma's new room. Looking down at the peaceful, sleeping
figure of her daughter, Susan felt almost unbearably in love with her.
Emma's little chest rose and fell, rose and fell. She had her father's
thick dark hair and big brown eyes, but her small frame and some-
times-playful/sometimes-hesitant spirit were all Susan.

   "Oh, sweet pea," she murmured. Gingerly she eased the covers
down from where Emma had tugged them up under her chin. She
insisted on being tucked in so tightly, even in the late-summer heat.

   Then Susan glanced at the window and gasped. "Oh God! *Oh*

my God!" she said, loudly, scaring herself in the quiet dark of the bed-room.

Emma stirred but didn't wake. Susan stepped closer to the win-dow and gaped, wide-eyed, at where a person, or the shadow of a person, was standing in the backyard, leaning against the rickety back fence and staring up. The man was massive. In his hand was the long barrel of a gun, or some kind of club, or . . . *something* . . . in the dark-ness, from this distance, it was impossible to say.

"Alex!" Susan shouted, but he didn't answer. Susan's heart was knocking at her ribs, and she clutched at the windowsill. "*Alex!* God damn it, *Alex!*"

Emma shifted and moaned in her sleep. Susan opened her mouth to scream again—she would have to go in there and shake him awake. But then she looked again, and there was nothing—no one—in the yard.

Whatever Susan had seen, or thought she had seen, it was gone.

4.

On Monday morning, exhausted from her nocturnal adventure and the fitful sleep that had followed, Susan sipped her coffee and scrolled through headlines on her iPhone while Emma toyed with her breakfast. When the nanny rang the bell at 8:50, a full twenty minutes late, Susan walked briskly down the hall to let her in, and a moment later Emma hopped down from the kitchen chair and flew into her arms.

"Marni! Marni! We live in *this* house now!"

"I know, buddy," said Marni, and swept the little girl up, mouthing "I am so sorry" to Susan over Emma's shoulder. Susan smiled forgivingly, boiling inside. Marni only worked from 8:30 until 2:30, and Susan counted on those hours, especially during a week like this one, when she had a million and a half things to do.

"The subways totally threw me for a loop," Marni apologized. "The Internet said it'd take me twenty-three minutes to get here, but it was at least twice that."

"That stinks," said Susan evenly, thinking *Wow, the Internet was wrong. Never could have been predicted.*

"Hey, the new place looks great," said Marni, and Emma dragged her by the hand to show her around.

Marni was a doctoral student in psychology at Fordham, finished with her coursework but still writing her dissertation, with mornings free and a need for extra cash. She had been working for them only about seven months—and had agreed, to Susan's mild chagrin, to stay in the job after their move. Marni's seeming inability to arrive on time was just one of several things that bothered Susan. She was, in general, a bit sloppy, leaving the lunch dishes in the sink and only occasionally bothering to clean the stroller and diaper bag before she left for the day.

There was also a collegiate looseness about Marni, an easy sexiness of tousled hair, multiple-pierced ears, and tight T-shirts that rubbed Susan the wrong way. She knew very little about Marni's personal life, but the young woman had never mentioned any particular boyfriend, and Susan had at some point decided that this indicated not chasteness but rather the opposite: an active and unsettled romantic and sexual life. Susan frequently imagined (and reprimanded herself for doing so) that Marni was coming to her nannying job directly from her latest one-night stand.

Alex's days started early, and he was usually gone before Marni arrived and home long after she left. He never paid any particular attention to her, which was just fine by Susan.

"So, Emma-roo," said Marni, tossing her little H&M jean jacket casually on top of a packing box as they returned from their circuit of the apartment. "Were you aware that Brooklyn has its very own children's museum?"

"It does? Let's go there! Let's go there!" Emma bounced around Marni in a loopy circle. "Mom! Mom! We're going to a children's museum!"

"Is that OK?" Marni asked Susan, who obviously couldn't say no, not now.

Oh, stop being so annoyed, Susan told herself, digging her wallet from her pocketbook to pay for museum admission and lunch. She wondered in passing whether her occasional distaste for Marni came from her own annoyance at herself, mild but ever-present: *you're not going to work, and we're* still *shelling out four hundred bucks a week for child care?*

She gave Emma a shower of kisses, handed Marni a pair of twenties, and headed out the door.

*

Susan's first stop was Trader Joe's, at the corner of Atlantic Avenue and Smith Street, so she could fill the fridge with milk and yogurt and stock the pantry with applesauce and juice boxes and cooking oil. Alex did most of the cooking, but Susan generally handled the shopping. She moved swiftly through the aisles, bopping her head to "Sugar Pie, Honey Bunch" and lingering briefly in the frozen meat section before adding FIND A BUTCHER to her to-do list and moving on. Next to Trader Joe's was a spacious wine shop run by twenty-something hipsters, where she picked up two reds and two whites from a "ten-and-under" table. "This Montepulciano is the *bomb*," said the girl behind the counter, who sported auburn pigtails, oversized plastic-framed glasses, and an arm sleeved with colorful tattoos. "Oh? Rad," said Susan, thinking, *I love Brooklyn.*

Back home, Susan unpacked the cold stuff and then took a half hour to line her drawers and cupboards with wax paper before unpacking the pantry items. She turned on the radio, found WNYC, and spent the rest of the Leonard Lopate Show slicing open boxes marked KITCHEN, rinsing off dishes they had stupidly packed in newsprint, and finding counter space for the KitchenAid, Cuisinart, and hand mixer. Settling down with her laptop at the kitchen table, Susan filled out a numbing series of address-change forms and then composed a mass e-mail with her new address, appending the de rigueur postscript about how "my cell phone number and e-mail will of course remain the same ... "

Susan's brisk march through her task list was slowed by a head-line on her Yahoo! homepage: Anna Mara Phelps, the young mother accused of killing her daughters, had been arraigned and pled not guilty by reason of insanity, as expected. Susan noted, before forcing herself to get back to work, that Phelps was a former actress, had moved to New York from Minneapolis in 2002, and was thirty-four years old, same as Susan.

Upstairs, Susan swept out the closet in the second bedroom and opened a box marked CLOTHES: EMMA. She was smoothing out the miniature party dresses on their pink plastic Cinderella hangers and arranging them carefully when she heard the excited clamor from downstairs, as Marni and Emma stomped inside. Downstairs she heard all about the Brooklyn Children's Museum, which apparently featured a working greenhouse, a delightfully scary collection of snakes, and a fully functional pretend pizza restaurant.

"And how was the bus ride back, sweets?" Susan asked, crouch-ing to wipe a smudge of yogurt from Emma's cheek.

"Oh, actually? She was super worn out," said Marni. "So we took a car home. I hope that's OK."

Susan went to find her purse, and forked over another nine bucks.

*

When Emma was up from her nap, Susan got her dressed and they went out together, with no fewer than three shopping lists: one for the hardware store, one for the drug store, and one marked "misc." On the front stoop, holding Emma in her arms and balancing the stroller on her back, Susan nearly tripped over Andrea, who was seated on the top step with her legs folded beneath her and the *Times* spread out on her lap.

"Whoa. God, sorry, Andrea."

"No, look at me, I couldn't be more in the way!"

Andrea was wearing oversized old-lady sunglasses, studded along the stems with rhinestones. Susan was always seeing glasses like them in secondhand shops and wishing she had the kitschy nerve to sport a pair. "So? Are we Brooklynites now? Are we finding everything OK?"

"I think so. Wait, no. Butcher?"

"Oh, yes. The place to go is called Staubitz. It's down Court Street, just past Kane, I think. Or just before. Anyway, it's down there somewhere. Should I draw you a map?"

"No, no."

Emma squirmed in her arms. "We're going, love. We're going."

"Some people like Los Paisanos, on Smith, but if you ask me those people are idiots. Staubitz is the place, and tell John I sent you."

"I will. Are you OK?"

She had noticed that Andrea was holding her hip, shifting her position laboriously from one buttock to the other.

"Oh, you know. This and that, dear. The equipment is old. Still works, but it's old." She gave Emma her big comedienne's wink, which Emma returned enthusiastically.

Susan smiled. "So, Staubitz?"

"Staubitz."

She gave Andrea a little mock salute and continued down the steps. Halfway down Cranberry Street, she remembered the person she'd seen, or maybe imagined seeing, lurking in the backyard on Sunday night, staring up at the house.

She stopped and turned back. "Oh, hey, Andrea?"

But the door was just closing; Andrea had slipped back inside.

*

Tuesday began on an unexpectedly delightful note: Emma woke up early, and Susan, feeling unusually well rested and at ease, decided they should whip up a batch of cookies. Emma, naturally, thought this was pretty much the best idea she'd ever heard. They spent a happy and loud half hour, clanging around the kitchen in matching polka-dot aprons, mixing, pouring, and giggling, until Alex came down for his coffee at 7:45 to find both wife and daughter flour-caked and giddy.

"Oo! They're ready! They're ready!" announced Emma, dancing in front of the oven while Alex yawned and scratched his butt.

Susan slipped on an oven mitt, pulled out the tray, and handed Emma a sample, which she ate in one bite before throwing her arms around her mother's waist. Susan sipped her own coffee, shot Alex a grin. "What can I say? The kid loves me."

Four hours later, Susan was bustling about in the master bedroom, hanging a few small framed photographs and waiting for the cable guy, when she was struck by a strong pang of guilt and self-recrimination.

It was all well and good to take on these endless logistical rounds—
shopping, unpacking, hanging pictures, hanging clothes—but when
was she going to set up her easel and do some painting?

That's right, mess around forever, whispered the accusatory inner
voice she knew too well, arch and recriminatory, *and then you never
have to put your money where your mouth is . . . right? Never have to try.*
Susan was frozen in place, holding her favorite red cardigan sweater
up by the arms like a dance partner; she had just dumped out an entire box of packed clothes that needed to be folded and put away.

Never try, never fail.

Susan knew what she should do: put down the sweater, march
downstairs, and start painting. No time like the present, right? There
was nothing she was doing that couldn't wait. Instead, she lay down
the sweater on the bed and brought its arms down and across, one by
one, then folded it deliberately upward from hem to collar, smoothed
the crease, and stowed it in the dresser.

Very nice, Frida Kahlo, said the voice of self-recrimination, soft
and insistent. *Very nice.*

*

The man from TimeWarner rang the bell at 11:58, two minutes before the expiration of the four-hour window in which the dispatcher
had prophesied his appearance. His name was Tony, and he made small
talk in a thick Brooklyn accent as he installed the cable box. Susan of-
fered coffee—"No, tanks," said Tony—and then hovered in the living
room, scanning the Arts section and waiting for him to finish.

"Hey," Tony said all of a sudden, and looked up from his squat
before the entertainment center. "Wassat?"

"What's what?" Susan asked.

"Dat. *Ping. Ping.* Hear dat?"

She narrowed her eyes and listened. It was very low, barely audible, but the cable guy was right: there was a light *ping,* every ten or fifteen seconds, coming from . . . somewhere. She walked a slow circle around the room, then up and down the hallway, but couldn't figure it out. "Weird," she said.

"Yeah," said the cable man. "Anyway, dat's it. Finished. Lemme show ya the remotes."

When Tony from TimeWarner was gone, Susan grabbed the dustpan and handbroom from under the kitchen sink and swept a tidy circle around the entertainment center, gathering up the little bits of clipped wire he'd left in his wake. Before she went back upstairs, she cast a quick, worried glance at the door to the bonus room.

"Tomorrow," she said firmly. "I'll do some painting tomorrow."

*

As was perhaps inevitable, given the speed with which Alex and Susan had decided to take the apartment on Cranberry Street, they started to discover small problems they had overlooked during their one brief tour. The face plate on an electric outlet in the kitchen was slightly askew, so Susan had to angle the prongs awkwardly to plug in the toaster. A long ugly crack marred the wall above the sink in the downstairs bathroom, and the faucet in the kitchen sink had to be tightened with unusual force, or it dripped.

And then, on Tuesday night, carrying Emma out of the bath in her oversized ducky towel, Susan jammed her big toe on a floorboard on the landing.

"Ow!" she shouted, "Damn it, damn it, damn it!"

Emma's eyes went wide. "Mama?"

"I'm OK, I'm OK, honey." She put Emma down and clutched at her throbbing toe like a cartoon character. "Alex, can you come up here, please?"

"Just a sec."

Examining the floor while Emma wrestled herself into her underpants, Susan discovered a slight but undeniable gapping between two of the floorboards. One of the boards was minutely raised, creating just enough of a little cliff to jam your toe against.

"We gotta be careful here," she said. "OK, Em?"

"Yeah," Emma agreed solemnly. "Careful."

"It's not a big deal," Alex concluded, when he took a look. "If we owned the place, maybe I'd pay someone to sand it out." Susan raised an eyebrow, and Alex shrugged. "Or whatever you do to floors. But I mean, whatever, I think we can just step around it."

"Yeah," said Susan. "I guess. But let's keep a lookout for other spots like that. I hadn't noticed it before, had you?"

"Nope."

Alex padded back down the stairs and returned to the living room, where he'd been basically camped out, staring at his computer screen, cutting and cropping digital images. It was a bummer to have him so distracted during their first week in a new home, but Susan understood the reason. GemFlex was a small company, and the only way they'd become a bigger one was by getting a "rep": a professional middleman who would tout their services to the big jewelry outfits, and handle all the negotiating and billing—all the tedious busywork that had the least relation to what Alex really enjoyed, which was taking pictures. Now there was a rep named Richard Hastie who'd called them, first thing Monday, with a week's worth of work for Cartier, shooting three watches for a small print advertisement. And though nothing had been stated explicitly, Alex and his partner felt they were being tried out, with the potential reward of not only steady work from Cartier, but ongoing representation from Hastie.

"So?" Susan ventured, hours later, when Emma was long asleep. She'd settled on the other end of the sofa, with a glass of wine and the crossword puzzle. "How's it going?"

"You know, I don't know," Alex answered slowly, looking up from his computer with a tired smile. "All right, I think."

"You think you'll get it?"

"Well, like I said, I don't know." He yawned and turned back to the screen. "I hope."

Susan returned to her puzzle, feeling a mild, prickly wash of irritation. Yes, he was busy, but it was unlike Alex not to say something along the lines of, "And how are *you* doing?" Never mind "the house looks great" or "thanks for working so hard to get us set up."

His focus on this opportunity actually frightened her a little, made her wonder how important this contract was to their financial health, especially after the considerable expense of the move.

Susan folded up her crossword and kissed Alex gently on the top of the head on her way upstairs.

*

Even after taking half an Ambien, Susan took what felt like an eternity to drift off, and when at last she did, it was into the grips of an awful nightmare. She was walking down Cranberry Street when she jammed her toe on a crack in the sidewalk, just as she had jammed it between the two floorboards on the landing. But this time the pain was intensified a hundredfold, out of all proportion to a stubbed toe, sending wave after wave of burning agony up her leg. Susan clutched at herself, howling, and went sprawling onto the sidewalk. Prostrate and writhing, she saw that Andrea Scharfstein was sitting at the top of the stoop, dressed in a wrap of eerily bright vermillion, waving her thin arms wildly, shouting, "Look out! Susan, *look out!*"

She craned her neck upward just in time to see a gigantic double stroller hurtling out of the sky. She leapt to her feet and stumbled back, and the carriage hit the sidewalk. The stroller exploded and blood burst out of it, as if the thing had been a gigantic sloshing balloon full of blood; erupting in waves of blood, cascades of it, vastly more blood than possibly could have been inside those two poor little girls. Susan was splattered, covered, drenched in blood. She wailed, wiping the blood from her eyes until she could see the small corpses of the girls, their battered pulpy skeletons, strapped into their little seats in the side-by-side double stroller, hands clenched together . . . she screamed again, woke herself with screaming, woke to find her hands balled into fists and grinding into her eyes.

Susan took a series of ragged breaths until her hands quit trembling. Then she staggered out of bed and into the bathroom and stared at herself in the mirror for a long time, wiping intensely at herself with her palms, as if the blood of the dream was still caked on her cheeks and clinging to her hair. At last she tiptoed back into the bedroom and stared at Alex, who slept peacefully, undisturbed. The glowing red lines of the bedside clock told her it was 5:42. Susan unplugged the baby monitor from the bedside table and took it downstairs, certain she was up for the day.

5.

Susan did not meet the "nice gentleman" who acted as Andrea's unofficial, part-time maintenance man until Wednesday afternoon.

It was a little after one, and Susan was returning from yet another epic morning of errands when she turned off Henry Street onto Cranberry and heard the panicked, terrified wailing of a child. Her heart lurched in her chest—*Emma*—and she burst into a panicked sprint, the heavy plastic-sheathed bulk of the dry cleaning shifting in the crook of her arm, shopping bags flapping against her legs.

Emma appeared to be unharmed, thank God. But the girl was red-faced and screeching, crying with a ferocity that Susan rarely witnessed, standing at the center of an anxious tableau at the bottom of the stoop, just past the squat black wrought-iron fence that separated the brownstone from Cranberry Street. Andrea was crouching beside the girl, patting her uneasily on the shoulder; Marni hovered over them, wringing her hands and looking around stupidly; a few steps to Marni's right, standing with one foot up on the bottom step, was an older black man with a bald pate and a massive gut, looking anxious and flustered. The sun glinted off the man's smooth scalp while trickles of sweat dripped into his eyes.

"Mama!" screeched Emma, holding out her thin little arms.

That's him, Susan thought as she launched herself into the scene and scooped up her daughter. *That's who I saw in the yard that night. That's him.* She cradled Emma to her chest and murmured, "Oh baby, oh baby, it's OK my love. It's OK." And then, to the rest of them: "What *happened*?"

"Emma got upset, the dear," said Andrea, straightening up and nervously readjusting the gold-grey kerchief knotted in her hair.

"I can see that. Why?"

"She was trying to get into the basement."

"What?"

Andrea gestured to a cramped plywood door under the steps, secured with a heavy padlock. Susan knitted her brow; she had never noticed the door before.

"I was upstairs, but I guess she was at the door to the basement, fussing with the lock, and Louis saw her and he rushed over to stop her." Susan looked at the stranger, who nodded steadily but said nothing, just pulled a handkerchief from his back pocket and ran it over his brow. "Which, in Louis's defense, he was absolutely right to do," Andrea continued. "That basement is no place for kids. Power tools, flammable materials—"

"Wait. Stop. Who is Louis?" Shifting Emma to her other arm, she pivoted toward the man. "Who are you?"

"Well, my name is Louis," he said slowly, and Susan rolled her eyes. *It's like an old-folks home around here.* "Yes. I got that."

"Louis is the gentleman I mentioned," Andrea said. "I told you. He handles things for me, repairs, blown fuses, light fixtures."

"Oh. Right. OK." To Susan, Louis seemed an extremely unlikely handyman: he was portly, to put it mildly, and looked like someone's kindly but absentminded great-uncle, emitting none of the quiet confidence Susan associated with mechanical aptitude. Plus, if the guy was any younger than Andrea, it was by five or ten years, tops; he looked like he would struggle to carry a bag of groceries, let alone haul a toolbox up the steep stairs of 56 Cranberry Street.

Emma's sobbing had subsided into a series of arrhythmic, pained hiccups; Susan squeezed her tighter and smoothed her pale hair.

"Did you *tell* her not to go down there, or did you raise your voice at her?" she demanded of Louis. "Did you *touch* her?"

"Oh, Lord, no," Louis said, shaking his head, aghast. "Absolutely not."

Andrea shook her head too, insistent, *no no no.* "Not Louis. He would not have put a hand on the child."

"Not in a million years," said Louis, shifting his stance and crossing his heavy arms across his stomach. Susan was not liking this—not one bit. *This* was the person who would come up to the apartment? To switch a fuse or unclog the toilet? Who would know what you're supposed to do about gapping floorboards? She turned to Marni. "And where were *you* during all this?"

"I was right here. I was fighting with the stroller." Marni fidgeted with the hem of her tight American Apparel T-shirt, looking like a child, ready to burst into tears. "She wandered away for two seconds, and the next thing I knew she was down there, and he was there. He wasn't yelling. He wasn't. He just spoke kind of, like, suddenly . . . " She glanced apologetically at Louis, who looked at the ground. "And I think that's what did it."

"You can't let her wander away."

"I know."

"For *any* seconds."

"I know. I'm really sorry."

Susan fought to stay calm, knowing that getting upset would

make it harder for Emma to regain her equilibrium. She turned back to Louis and forced a smile.

"Well, it's not a big deal. I'm sure you didn't mean it. Anyway, nice to meet you."

Louis grinned, relieved. "Likewise. Any friend of Andrea's."

"Right. But can I ask you one more thing?"

"Of course. Anything you like."

"Were you standing in the yard last Sunday night? Right after we moved in?" As she was asking the question, Susan realized how strange it sounded—strange, or accusatory. "Like, looking up at the bedroom window? For some reason?"

"No." Louis shook his big head, and turned to Andrea. "I most certainly was not."

"OK," said Andrea, and Susan nodded. "OK."

Louis retreated to the backyard, and the rest of them tromped in a ragged line to the top of the stoop, Susan hugging Emma to her chest, Marni struggling behind with the pile of dry cleaning and the other bags, the carry-strap of the collapsed strolled looped across her chest.

"Did you find Staubitz the other day?" Andrea called, a few steps behind.

"Yeah," said Susan, not looking back. "I found it."

From the top of the stoop, Susan peered over the side at the door that had been the source of the morning's drama. It had a foreboding, dilapidated appearance, old and half rotted and probably laced with termites. The door itself didn't look safe for kids, let alone whatever power tools and flammables were padlocked behind it. Whatever Louis's story was, Susan concluded, it was a good thing he had warned Emma away from that door.

"Everything's OK, my love," she told her daughter again, feeling the wet warmth of the girl's breath as she snuggled into her throat. "Everything's OK."

*

Once they were inside, Susan told Marni she could go ahead and get going.

"Susan, I am really, really sorry about that. It won't happen again. Seriously." Susan glanced at Emma, who had wiped the last of the tears from her eyes and was settled on a kitchen chair, flipping through an Elephant and Piggie book called *I Love My New Toy*.

"All right, Marni."

"I'm serious."

"I know you are," Susan replied flatly, not ready to let the girl off the hook. "Thanks."

A couple minutes after Marni left, Andrea was at the door, her headscarf retied and her big old-lady sunglasses pushed up over her hair. She was smiling sheepishly, a girlish affectation that was slightly ghastly on her age-lined face, and bearing an old-fashioned toy: a wooden stick attached to a rolling chamber full of little plastic balls that popped and danced when you pushed it.

Emma looked up immediately. "Is that for me?"

"First you say hi, honey," said Susan, wearily. She'd had more than enough of Andrea for today.

Andrea laughed and handed over the toy. "Now, Susan, listen," she said, "I feel just awful over what happened, I do, and I wanted to say again how sorry I am."

"It's fine, Andrea."

"And for the record, Louis is a very good person. Absolutely a gentleman. He doesn't look like much, but he gets the job done. You've got my word on it."

Emma scooted past, pushing her new popper toy, howling with pleasure as the balls danced in the chamber. Susan smiled at her little girl's happiness; Andrea, smiling too, laid a spidery hand across Susan's upper arm.

"Now, isn't that the most darling thing?" she said. "My Howard, he just loved toys. He used to buy old ones and restore them, then we'd give them out at Christmas to the kids in the neighborhood. He had all sorts of hobbies, Howard did. Toys. Trains. Civil War. A man of wide-ranging and restless intelligence, my Howard."

"Sounds like he was quite the catch."

"Oh, forget it," Andrea growled with sudden sharpness, waving her hand angrily, as if dismissing an unpleasant topic that Susan had brought up. "We don't have to talk about *him*."

Whoa, thought Susan. *What just happened?*

But just as quickly as the overlay of anger had entered Andrea's voice, it disappeared, and the old lady grinned engagingly. "Anyway, I thought Emma would like the toy."

On cue, Emma crashed the push-toy into the kitchen wall, squealed with delight, and executed a wobbly three-point turn. "Thanks, Andrea. It's really very sweet."

Andrea waved away the thanks. "Just one more thing. About the basement."

"I know. Stay out of the basement. We got it." She needed to get Emma her lunch and put her down for a nap. The truth was, Susan felt like she could use a little nap of her own.

"No, it's just, I keep forgetting to mention. Go ahead and bring any biodegradable trash to the bottom of the stoop, or even just out-side my door, downstairs. Fruit and veggie peels, eggshells, teabags, coffee grounds. I'll take it down to the basement for composting."

"Sure, Andrea. That's fine."

"And that's just one more reason we want the little one to steer clear of the basement. Stinks something awful, it really does. Two big fifty-five-gallon drums of decaying trash. No fit playground for our little duck, right?"

"Right."

After she had tucked Emma in for her nap, Susan paused at the window to close the shade and saw Louis on his hands and knees at the edge of the garden. He was hunched over and drenched in sweat, grunting with the effort of tugging free the weeds. She watched for a moment, to see if he'd look up, but he did not.

Susan tugged down the shade, whispered "good nap" to Emma, and shut the door.

6.

Marni, no doubt shaken by Susan's anger and thinking her gig might be on thin ice, showed up the following morning at 8:22 with a comprehensive vision for the day. "I thought, as long it's still so hot, I could take Emma down to that park at the end of Atlantic Avenue, the one that's got all the water slides and sprinklers?"

"Sure." Susan smiled at Marni's puppy-dog eagerness to please. She hoped she hadn't been *too* harsh with her the day before.

"And we can get lunch out, if it's OK?" Marni's auburn hair was swept up in a thick pile on top of her head. "My friend Lucy, who sits for these twins in Park Slope, told me about this place right on Atlantic called the Moxie Spot, where you can get grilled cheese, sweet-potato fries, that kind of stuff."

"Sounds good to me," said Susan, brushing a tangle out of Emma's hair with her Dora the Explorer brush. "Does that sound good to you, Emma Loo Hoo?"

It sounded very good to Emma, judging by the speed with which she bolted up the stairs to get ready, Marni chasing after to find her swimsuit.

"Lots of sunscreen, please!" Susan called up the steps.

When the girls had gone, Susan put her coffee cup in the sink and stood motionless in the kitchen for a long moment, looking out the window. On Cranberry Street, the first leaves were beginning to turn, with striking bursts of orange appearing amid the clusters of green. A squirrel leaped daringly from an upmost branch to a telephone line, sending a shower of acorns down from the tree and a ripple down the line.

This was it. There was nothing else to do. Small tasks, of course, still clung stubbornly on the to-do list: she needed a couple new coat hangers to replace those broken in the move, for example, and at some point she would need to dig out a flathead screwdriver and tighten that loose outlet cover above the kitchen counter, or get Alex to do it. But all the big things and urgent things had been accomplished. Their renter's insurance policy and newspaper delivery and banking statements had been transferred to the new address; the shower curtains and mirrors had been hung; the furniture was in place and all the lamps had been reunited with their bulbs.

Susan took a deep breath and strode down the long front hallway like a toreador. There was a single box still sitting unopened beside the doorway to the bonus room; inside were her brushes, rolled-up canvases, and a fresh tin of oil paints. She lifted the box, tucked it under one arm, and pulled open the door. A strong reek of cat piss, warm and cloying, came rolling out, and Susan coughed.

"Oh, God," she said, pinching closed her nose. "What the hell?"

Susan put down the box and sniffed again, gingerly, then recoiled and clamped her hand over her face. It was urine, definitely, a thick gross cloud of pee-stink, coming in waves from the bonus room. How could she not have noticed a smell like that before? And then Susan remembered the fleeting moment when she *had* noticed it, when her powerful, almost supernatural tug of love for the apartment had been briefly troubled by a bad smell from this room. But

it couldn't have been as strong as this, could it? Had something happened since they moved in?

Wouldn't that just serve her right: while she was procrastinating,
avoiding her supposedly beloved art, some ungodly stench had been
festering in her beautiful new studio.

It's my own fault! Susan thought, banging her fists against her
thighs. *My own fault!*

Tears trembled in her eyes, and she ordered herself to chill. *It's just
not that big a deal.* Breathing through her mouth, Susan walked briskly
across the bonus room and opened the window. It slid up easily, but
then the top of the window banged against the frame, and it slid right
back down.

"Oh, come on," Susan muttered. She tried again, sliding the window up and watching it sail back down again, as if blocked by a hidden hand determined to keep it shut, to let no air into the stale and
stagnant room.

"Crapola," Susan muttered.

First the delightful fragrance of cat urine, now a defective window. Her mind ran to the separating floor boards on the second-
floor landing and the spooky Door to Perdition under the front
stoop. *Anything else we overlooked?* she thought bitterly. *Railroad tracks
running through the kitchen? Faucets spraying fire?*

Susan stomped back to the kitchen for a wooden chair. She
dragged it back down the long hallway, through the living room, and
into the bonus room, feeling damp pockets of sweat open up in her
armpits. She pushed the chair into place and climbed up to examine
the window frame, not sure exactly what she was looking for. She saw
what Andrea had meant about the windows being double-paned
against the noise—there was a second pane of glass set in the window,

separated by a thin millimeter of space from the frame. But did that explain the . . .

Oh. Here we go.

There was a thin gash dug into the wood at the top of the window. And buried in the wood, sticking up just enough to keep the window from kissing closed into the frame, was a folded piece of paper.

No, not a piece of paper. It was a photograph.

Susan dug the picture free from the wood and turned it over in her hand. It was a wallet-sized snapshot that had been folded over twice into a fat little square, like a middle-school crush note. She sat down on the chair and unfolded the photograph slowly, carefully tugging it loose from itself; the back, it seemed, had been coated with some sort of adhesive. When she had it open she forgot about getting the window open, forgot even about the foul reek of the room. She sat in the high-backed kitchen chair and gazed at the happy couple in the picture.

They were cuddled together in a red-curtained photo booth, the old-fashioned kind that was set up sometimes in movie theater lobbies or as a fun activity at a wedding reception. The man in the picture was short haired and goateed, sporting a fedora and a pair of those dark, horn-rimmed Elvis Costello–style glasses so favored by hipster dudes. He was planting a fat smooch on the woman's cheek. She was pretty and pert nosed, wearing a teasing, sexy grin. Her hair was dyed a bold scarlet, with bangs slashed at a fashionable angle across her eyes.

Cute, thought Susan. She turned the picture over, looking for a date, or names, anything jotted on the back. She found instead that the adhesive coating the back of the picture was, in fact, dried blood, tiny bits of which flaked off in her hand. And, at the dead center, was the dark, crusted swirl of a bloody thumbprint.

*

"Hey, Andrea? Did the people who lived here before us have a cat?"

Andrea's Scharfstein's eyes went wide, and she stopped what she was doing, which was spooning sugar out of a powder-blue ceramic bowl into Susan's mug.

"A cat?" she said at last, with an intensity that made Susan feel a little unsettled. Andrea's hand trembled slightly as she returned the miniature spoon into the sugar bowl. "Why do you ask?"

Susan had only wanted to ask her question and get back upstairs, but Andrea had been so nakedly delighted at the unexpected visit that she decided a quick cup of tea wouldn't kill her. Andrea sang lightly to herself as she moved slowly from living room to kitchen and back, preparing a tea service, fruit plate, and cookie tray.

"Can I help you?" Susan had asked, but Andrea had waved her off, relishing the role of hostess. "No, you sit, dear, you sit. I'm quite all right. Fine and dandy like sugar candy."

Andrea's apartment was laid out on the same blueprint as the first floor of Alex and Susan's, with the kitchen at one end and the living room at the other, though it could not have been decorated more differently. Where Susan strove for a clean, modern, and uncluttered aesthetic, Andrea's rooms were stuffed with oversized wooden furniture, tottering bookshelves, potted plants, and—in one corner of the living room—a glass case displaying a collection of hideous "ethnic" dolls. On the opposite wall, Andrea had hung vertical mirrors on either side of the air shaft; an effort, Susan suspected, to downplay the presence of the unusual, semi-industrial architectural feature. There was nothing, Susan mused, to indicate the influence of a second aesthetic, nothing to suggest that a man had ever lived here; she wondered when it was that the late great Howard had passed away.

Andrea's eyes looked tired and rheumy as she raised her teacup to her lips, and Susan felt like she could see past the makeup and the bright clothes to Andrea's real age, the fragility of a woman in her early or mid-seventies—and, chillingly, felt she could see past *that*, too, to the very old woman that Andrea would soon be: a few lank hairs clinging to an ancient scalp, the skin pulled taut around the skull.

"I'm sorry to say this," Susan said. "But that small room behind the living room? The one you called the bonus room? It smells really bad. Like cat pee."

"Cat pee." Andrea exhaled heavily and placed a hand to her forehead. "It's worse than that, Susan."

"What do you mean?"

"I am so sorry about this. I thought we had got that smell out, I really did."

"Andrea?" It was like one of those old grosser-than-gross riddles from elementary school. *What's grosser than a room soaked in cat urine?* Susan sipped from her steaming cup of tea and stared at Andrea, waiting for the answer.

"They were a young couple. The previous tenants, I mean. Jack and Jessica, though she went by Jessie. Sweet names, right? I liked to tease them about it, tell them it oughta be up in lights: Jack and Jessie! Jessie and Jack! In their twenties, I think, and not married. 'Living in sin,' we used to call it, not that it was any of my business."

Susan thought of the photograph of the sweet kids, posing

giddily for the camera. The picture was currently lying on her kitchen table, faceup.

"Jessica Spender was her name. His surname, I must say I never knew. She signed the lease and wrote the rent checks, too—again, not that it was any of my business. And they had a cat. It was the sweetest little thing, barely more than a kitten. Catastrophe, they called her. Catastrophe the cat."

Susan smiled faintly at the name, sipped her tea. Naming a cat Catastrophe, a gesture at once mildly ironic and sweet, the hallmarks of the generation just younger than her own.

"Anyway, Jess and Jack were not to be, apparently. They seemed very loving to me, very happy, but I guess appearances can be deceiving, because one day Jack abruptly departed. As in, one morning he was just, you know, poof. Gone. And I found poor Jess on the stoop outside, crying and crying. I mean—she was—couldn't even speak. It was really something."

"Yikes."

Andrea took a deep, ragged breath, coughed drily, and shook her head. "Well, before you get too sympathetic. Jessie left, too, shortly thereafter, stiffing yours truly for a month's rent. Only reason I knew she was gone was because the check never showed up. A couple days I don't mind, of course. Between you and me, I won't starve. But two weeks, then it's three weeks, it's a problem. And you know, as the days go by, I don't see her, I'm worried. So I knocked one day, then let myself in. And . . . "

Andrea stopped, shaking her head with tight, birdlike jerks. A watery pain had entered her voice, and Susan leaned across the table and stroked the older woman's rough, papery hand—all the while dying of curiosity.

"And . . . " she prompted.

"And the poor cat was dead in that little room. I guess, in her hurry to get out, Jessica had—had forgotten and closed that door . . . no food, or no water. And this was July, remember. It would get extremely hot in there with the air off and the window closed. The poor animal . . . "

Andrea squeezed her eyes shut against the memory, and Susan found herself a bit choked up as well. *Poor Catastrophe! Poor little kitten! How could anybody . . . God. People are horrible.*

Andrea honked loudly in a napkin. "Anyway," she said firmly, as if to clear the air of the unpleasantness. "Louis and I cleaned the area thoroughly, but I guess not thoroughly enough. I will certainly have him come up and take another pass."

"That would be great. Whenever he gets a chance."

"No, not 'whenever he gets a chance,'" said Andrea, and then craned around, raising her voice. "Louis?"

"Just one moment," came the booming reply. Susan, startled, half rose, looking around. The whole time they'd been sitting there, she'd heard not a sound from anywhere else in the apartment, and Andrea had given no indication they weren't alone. Now Louis, in thick black boots and a denim work shirt, emerged from the front of the apartment.

"What's up?"

"That nasty odor is still hanging around the little room upstairs."

"You're kidding me. Really?"

Susan nodded. "Sorry."

"No, no, don't be sorry. *I'm* sorry." Louis stroked his chin. "OK if I come by tomorrow?"

"Sure."

"What time works?"

"Early is good, just in terms of—"

"Early is fine," he said. "What time are you up and about?"

"We have a three-and-a-half year old, so, I mean, we're up at seven. But—"

"No problem. I'll be there at 7:30. Just gotta put it in the old bean." Louis chuckled, tapping at his forehead, and then headed back down the hallway, murmuring to himself. "Seven-thirty . . . seven-thirty . . ."

"He's working on the sink in the bathroom, which is clogged like you wouldn't believe," Andrea explained and then leaned forward and adopted a confidential, just-us-ladies tone. "Hairballs."

"Ah," said Susan. What else could one say to such a thing? Andrea rose with a sigh to clear away the teacups.

Susan thought about poor Catastrophe, and about Jack and Jessica, who had so thoughtlessly left the animal behind. Who, Susan wondered, had stuffed that picture in the window frame, before their abrupt disappearance? Who had clutched that photograph with a bloody thumb?

"Enjoy that gorgeous hair of yours while you can, dear," said Andrea wistfully from the kitchen, and Susan self-consciously brought a hand up to her dirty-blonde curls. "Because when you get old, it will fall out in clumps. In *clumps*."

Susan rose abruptly, thanked Andrea for the tea, and went back upstairs.

7.

Susan had forgotten entirely about the faint pinging sound the cable man had brought to her attention on Tuesday morning. But on Thursday night Alex heard it, too. Dinner was over, and the whole family was smooshed on the leather living-room sofa, reading *Amelia Bedelia*, when he paused midsentence and said, "Do you hear that?"

"Hear what?"

"Dada? Read, please."

"One sec, hon."

"Hear what, Al?"

"Read the book, dada."

Then they all heard it, faint but distinct, sounding from some-where and nowhere. *Ping.* And then a few seconds later, again: *ping.* They slid off the couch, all three of them, and started meandering around the house searching for the source of the noise.

"Could it be the smoke alarm?" Susan ventured. "Carbon monoxide?"

"No way," said Alex, glancing up at the light on the smoke de-tector, which glowed an unbroken green. "Alarms better be a lot louder than that."

Ping went the noise again, so soft you almost couldn't hear it. Emma said, "Ping!" in return and then started bouncing up and down, yelping, "Ping! Ping!"

"Ping!" shouted Alex, and then the noise sounded again, as if in response: *ping*. "Weird," he said. "It's like sonar."

Ping went the house, and Emma went, "Ping!" and they all giggled.

Their search was fruitless, and the noise stopped, and Alex chased Emma up the stairs for bath. Later, after their daughter was asleep, Susan was about to tell Alex about the cat-pee smell, and the awful story of Jack and Jessica and Catastrophe the cat, and the photograph with the bloody thumbprint on the back. But she checked herself, realizing with a prickly flush of shame that the story would have to begin with an explanation of why today was the first time she had set foot in her "studio" since they moved in.

She stood in silence, leaning on the kitchen counter, watching Alex gather lettuce, cucumber, tomato, and red onion from the fridge to start on a salad, imagining his response:

"Well, honey, I thought the whole point of moving was so that you could have your own space to paint?"

"Well, honey, if you're not painting and you're not watching Emma, then what are you doing?"

"Well, honey, what the hell?"

Susan shook her head clear, pulled a knife from the block, and helped him cut vegetables. During dinner she related a funny gossip item she'd read on a fine-arts blog, about one of the big Chelsea gallery owners and his ever-changing lineup of buxom "assistants." But Alex's responses were polite and peremptory, and as soon as they were done eating he turned to his computer and the barrage of e-mails he needed to send to prepare for tomorrow. Apparently there had been a screwup that day on the Cartier shoot, when a watch face was scratched by a worthless lighting assistant that Vic had hired for cheap. It was a major setback, and Susan could tell that Alex was deeply worried.

When she went upstairs to sleep, Alex remained in the living room, muttering to himself and tapping away.

*

Louis arrived to clean the smell from the bonus room at precisely 7:30 the next morning.

"Will wonders never cease," Susan murmured at the sound of his knock at the door before calling out "just a sec," pulling her robe close to her chest, and opening the door. Alex had left fifteen minutes earlier, grimly clutching his travel coffee mug, game face on for a trying day. After offering Louis coffee or tea, which he cheerfully declined, Susan got Emma going on breakfast and then stood awkwardly in her bathrobe in the doorway of the bonus room, unable to decide if it made her more uncomfortable to perch there—watching an elderly man on hands and knees, in his jeans and an undershirt, cleaning her floor—or to return to the kitchen and leave him alone in this isolated corner of her home.

"Have you been working for Andrea a long time?" she asked.

"Well, how's forty years?" Louis looked over his shoulder with a broad, playful grin. "Would you call that a long time?"

"Forty years?"

"I kid you not. Well, now, I guess I've only been *working* for her, officially, since Howard passed away. Helping out with the odd jobs and what-have-you. Do everything I can for her, you know?"

Susan nodded as Louis settled back on his haunches, sponge

dripping idly onto the hardwood. The guy was a talker, that was clear.

"I've been retired some years now, so I've got my days free. Thirty-seven years as the assistant principal at Philippa Schuyler, up on Greene Avenue. And I tell you, after all those years keeping tabs on a couple hundred young people, scrubbing the occasional floor, well, I call that a vacation." Louis's laugh was low, gentle, and melodious, a slow-played tympani drum roll: *huh-huhm, huh-huhm, huh-huhm*. "No, but I loved it, I did. Loved those kids."

Susan thought with fondness of the assistant principal at her own middle school back in New Jersey. Mr. Crimson. Clemson? Something like that.

"You want to know the truth, I've known Howard and Andrea since 1970, if you can believe that. Autumn of 1970. We met right here in Brooklyn, protesting over Kent State, waving our signs in Cadman Plaza. One day I'll bring up some pictures. As Andrea might say, you will *plotz*."

He gave the Yiddish word a thick, comical Andrea-style growl, and Susan smiled. "And when did Howard pass away?"

The pleasant grin slipped from Louis's face, and he looked down at the floor. "Four years ago. And may God rest his poor unfortunate soul."

A deep silence welled up, and Louis turned back to scouring the floor. As Susan watched him, she felt a twinge of remorse for the way she had sized him up yesterday: though he was clearly no kind of professional handyman, he was forceful and competent as he went about his business in the small room. He focused his efforts on no specific spot, just blasted away at the whole floor with bleach and Pine-Sol, inch by inch, the shock-and-awe cleaning method.

After a few moments, Emma called out from the kitchen.

"Mama?" she said. "All done."

"OK, baby." From the kitchen came the scrape of a chair leg and a gentle thud as Emma lowered herself to the floor. Susan smiled: *she's growing up so fast.* Louis's memories, his nostalgic attitude, had put her in a sentimental frame of mind. *My little girl.*

"Hey. Uh, Susan?" She turned and saw that Louis had shifted up onto his knees and was now hauling himself laboriously to his feet. He crossed his arms over his sizable stomach and stood with evident nervousness, not meeting her eye. "Something I need to say to you."

"All right."

"I wasn't looking in your little girl's room. That night. I need you to know that."

"Yes," she replied, taken aback. "You said."

There was an adamance in this declaration, a pleading quality, as if Louis was sickened by the idea of anyone thinking even for a moment that he was the kind of person who would peep at a child. Susan believed him.

"But . . . "

"But?"

"I *was* standing out there. I like to keep an eye on Andrea. Just between you and me, Susan, I get a little . . . just a little worried about the old girl, sometimes."

"Worried?"

Louis looked around, discomfort emanating like sweat, his big hands knotted together. "Yeah. Since Howard died, she hardly sleeps, you know, and that's not right. She seems . . . oh, just sad, I guess. Tell you the truth, this house has always had an *atmosphere* to it. Something. Just a whole lot of sadness in the place since Howard died. So sometimes I peek in on old Andrea. Just keepin' tabs. Figure I owe it to my friend."

"Huh." Susan wasn't sure what she thought about this information. A brief, painful surge of memory coursed through her, of her mother, her mother's death, the stupid funeral. *They had tried to make her look, right in the casket, but for God's sake . . .*

"And, if you don't mind my asking," Susan said suddenly. "What was it Howard died of, exactly?"

"No, I don't mind." Louis heaved a big, body-shifting sigh, juggled the bucket of supplies from one hand to another. Now the room smelled thickly of cleaning fluids, of bleach and ammonia. "He was sick. Real sick. It came on sudden, because before that, I tell you straight up, this was the healthiest person you could ever meet. We played racquetball three times a week, and if I beat him once in forty years, I can't say when it was."

"Wow." Susan was blatantly prying now, but she couldn't help it. "What did he have?"

"I don't exactly know. A disease. Something in his blood. He didn't let it kill him, though. That was not Howard's style." Louis tilted his head to one side, his eyes glinting with the memory of his friend. "He shot himself, you see? Did himself in before the disease could do it first. Shot himself right in the head."

*

In the front hall, Emma eyed Louis warily, but he crouched down, tugging up the cuffs of his jeans, and grinned at her. "Hey, little sister, can I tell you a secret? I got a granddaughter just your age, and you want to know her name? Her name is Amethyst."

Emma's eyes widened, and she nodded, as if, yes, she *had* known that. "And guess what?" she asked, leaning confidentially toward Louis. "That's a kind of jewel."

"No kidding!" He pretended astonishment, and Emma nodded rapidly, beaming. "It is! It's a jewel. And it's *purple.*"

As Louis stood up, a faint but clear *ping* filled the room.

"Ping!" Emma yelped merrily in reply.

"That's—" Susan began, but Louis held up one hand, palm up, listening. "Hold on."

It went again. *Ping.*

And then, a moment later, came a ghostly, deflating moan, raspy, long and low. It was an ugly, uncanny noise, all the more so for being so indistinct—barely audible, really, and originating, or so it felt, from no particular place. Louis narrowed his eyes, took a halting step in no particular direction, then stopped. Susan reached for Emma and grasped her hand. She held her breath, waiting for the noises to come again, felt her whole body grow thick with tension and unease.

A second passed, then another. Silence.

And then her iPhone rang, ripping through the silence, and Susan screamed.

8.

"Marni," said Susan into the phone. "Crap, you scared me."

"Why? What?"

"Mama?" said Emma. "What's crap?"

"Nothing, love. Marni, what's up?" Susan glanced at the clock on the cable box: 8:17. Marni was supposed to be walking through the door in thirteen minutes. Louis gave a cheerful salute and mouthed "so long." Susan held up a finger for him to wait—*the pinging noise, what about*—but it was too late.

"Listen," Marni said. "I am really sorry about this . . . "

Speaking in a voice so exaggeratedly throaty and congested that Susan immediately suspected playacting, Marni explained that she'd felt ill last night, hoped it would fade by this morning, but woken just as bad. Of course she would come in anyway, knowing how much Susan had to do, but the last thing she wanted was for Emma to catch anything from her.

"Sure, sure," said Susan, only half listening to Marni's elaborate apologies. "All right, then. Feel better."

She hung up, took a deep breath, and called out, "Guess what, Emma? Looks like it's an all-day mama day!"

"Really? Yay!"

Emma bounced up the stairs to her bedroom to get dressed

while Susan chastised herself for feeling irritated. After all, it'd been ages since she'd spent a whole day with her spirited, funny little daughter, just the two of them. *Come on*, she told herself, turning her back on her studio and heading up the stairs. *We'll have a blast.*

While Emma rifled through her drawers, loudly considering different possible outfits, Susan waited on the landing between the bedrooms and examined the floorboards.

The gap, that little crack . . . was it widening? She hadn't measured, of course, and it was still an infinitesimal separation, but she felt sure it was slightly bigger. The wood was groaning, separating, or whatever it was that wood did. *I'll get Louis back up here*, Susan thought. *Maybe he can take care of it.*

*

According to 1010 WINS, the morning would be rain streaked but the afternoon clear, so Susan decided she and Emma would start their day at the small branch library in Cadman Plaza before lunch and then head to Pierrepont Playground after nap. On the way to the library, Susan left a message for Alex, letting him know that Marni had bailed, so if there was any way he could get home earlier than usual, she'd appreciate the relief. An hour passed, and then two, as Susan and Emma read picture books and put Dora the Explorer through her paces on the ancient desktop computer in the children's section. Susan became more and more irritated with Alex's failure to return her call—she knew he was busy, trying to repair the damage done by the lighting assistant and salvage the crucial Cartier shoot. But he could at least check in, to acknowledge the change in schedule. The morning slipped by, they went home for lunch, and still Alex didn't call.

He must be really busy, Susan told herself. *He must be slammed.*

"Mama? You OK, Mama?"

"Yes, love. Eat your sandwich."

While Emma napped, Susan ate her own lunch, a bagel with cream cheese from a place on Montague Street, and flipped aimlessly through the paper. There was an article in the New York section about a co-op board on the Upper West Side dealing with a bedbug infestation: a couple was protesting an edict they'd received to either undergo a costly extermination or move. Susan skimmed the article before flipping to the crossword. When she went to the junk drawer for a pen, she found the photograph of Jessie Spender and her boyfriend Jack.

Such a shame, she thought, turning the picture over in her hands in the light of the kitchen window. *They look so happy.*

After nap, at the playground, they ran into Shawn, the sweet-faced kid with the cornrows whom Emma had played tag with on the Promenade, the morning they first came to look at the apartment. While the children played an elaborate game of Cinderella, in which they took turns in the roles of prince, princess, fairy godmother, and coach-bearing horse, Susan chatted with the boy's mother, Vanessa.

"Oh, hey, have you got Shawn in a preschool?"

"Three days a week. If you need any information on what's around, just ask. I did so much research it's ridiculous. I'm way anal about that stuff."

Susan grinned—Vanessa sounded like a woman after her own heart. "I will *totally* take you up on that," she said. The woman agreed to arrange a play-date-slash-information-session sometime soon, and they swapped numbers.

Soon after Vanessa and Shawn's departure, Susan and Emma's pleasant afternoon was marred by an ugly incident. A tall, coolest-dad-at-the-playground kind of character, in a tailored sport coat and black jeans, eyes locked on his BlackBerry as he pushed his daughter on the swing, gave the girl a too-hard shove and sent her flying. The kid, a frail, dark-haired girl of five or six, landed headfirst on a jutting edge of rock and came up wailing, gushing blood. The mother ran over from a bench while the father furtively jammed his Black-Berry in his pocket.

"Can I get you something?" Susan called out, lifting Emma from her swing and rushing over. "Does she need a bandage? Should we call an ambulance?"

The mother didn't respond, focused on the girl, cradling her head and daubing at the cut with a wet paper towel. Mr. BlackBerry, however, turned to Susan with open irritation. "An ambulance?" he said. "No, it's nothing. She'll be fine."

It didn't look like nothing to Susan, but it was also none of her business.

"Is she OK?" asked Emma, craning around in her stroller seat, as Susan wheeled her out the gates of the playground.

"Yes, doll," said Susan. "Of course."

Susan cast her own glance backward at the frightened girl, who was rising unsteadily, reddish streaks caked to her forehead. She thought of the awful dream she'd had the other night: The stroller slamming into the ground and bursting like a bomb, sending fountains of blood spraying into the sky. She thought of the rusty smudge on the back of the photograph; she thought of poor Catastrophe the cat, starving and mad in the bonus room, white spit and pink blood foaming the corners of his mouth.

*

"Alex? Hey."

They had just returned home, and Susan answered her iPhone on the first ring. It was 4:45 p.m.

"Hey, babe. How are you?"

"I called this morning. Did you get my message?"

"What? Yeah. Oh—I mean, I think so. This morning?"

Alex's voice carried an undertone, a subtle tightness, indicating to Susan that he was looking at his computer while they talked. Vic was shouting orders to someone in the background.

"You sound busy."

"Susan, I'm sorry about this, but I can't come home tonight."

"Oh." Susan felt a queer twisting in her gut. She cradled the phone under her ear while she sat Emma down to tug off her shoes.

"It's this stupid watch. It took us all morning to find a new face and get it affixed properly. Now we still have to shoot the thing, along with the sport watch, the Rolex, the one that was actually scheduled for today. It's gonna be hours."

"How many hours?" Susan struggled to control her voice.

"I really have no idea, babe."

"Oh." Susan paused. How understanding was she supposed to be here? "So, you know, Marni didn't come in today."

"Seriously?"

"Yeah, I told you on the message."

"Hold on." He yelled to someone in the room with him, probably Vic: "Two seconds, OK? One second?" Then he was on the phone again. "That sucks. I'm sorry about this. We really have to nail this gig. You know that, right?"

Exactly how bad *was* Alex's business these days, Susan wondered. She felt a dark pocket of despair open in her stomach: they'd just blown all this money on the move, increased their rent . . . what if Alex's business was about to crumble? Then what? *You can always go back to Legal Aid, pick up law-temp work, document review . . . something. . . .*

"Listen, Sue, I gotta go."

"Sure, sure."

She hung up, lowered the phone, and saw her daughter staring at her, her eyes quivering saucers of grief.

"Honey?"

Emma burst into tears. "I wanted to talk to daddy!"

*

Three and a half hours later, with Emma sleeping soundly, Susan fixed herself an easy dinner of pasta and a glass of shiraz. Then she washed the dishes, cleared the table, and dug the picture of Jessica and Jack out of the junk drawer. She walked straight into the bonus room, set up her easel, and tacked the photograph in the lower-right-hand corner of a fresh canvas. The cat-pee stink was gone, thank God, but Susan left the window open anyway, allowing the mild nighttime chill of early fall to breathe into the room. There were two electrical outlets, and in one Susan plugged the baby monitor so she could hear if Emma cried; in the other she plugged her laptop, so she could turn on iTunes and listen to Bach's *Mass in B Minor*, always her favorite music to paint to.

Susan arranged her pleasingly old-fashioned wooden palette, her turpentine, her cleaning rags, her wineglass, and the bottle of Shiraz.

"All right," Susan said to the photograph of Jessica Spender.

"Shall we?"

Slowly at first, she painted. Her eyes darted back and forth between the photograph and her canvas as she scumbled in the thin oval of Jessica Spender's face, the high angles of her cheekbones, two dark recesses for the eyes, the confident angle of the hairline. Soon Susan was working faster, shedding her initial hesitance, losing herself in the work, drawing in details with the tip of a brush. She sang along with the music, moving her brush confidently, slashing and darting, feeling a kind of vigorous animal power flowing through her as she attacked the canvas.

Occasionally, Susan danced backward to survey her work, grunted approvingly, took a gulp of her wine, and dove back in. *I'm good at this*, she thought, jabbing her brush at the portrait and then yelping aloud. "I'm fucking *great!*"

Burning hot, sweating buckets, Susan stripped down to her bra and underwear, kept painting, faster and faster, her eyes locked on Jessica's eyes, hypnotized by the woman she was bringing to life on canvas. She disappeared into the work, edging in the dark shapes, thickening her layers, massaging the colors, feeling the power of each small act of creation. The *Mass* crescendoed, the Credo, and Susan moaned with exultation, lost to the world.

When she heard the knock at the door, her hands froze. She looked around wildly, heaving breath, scared and guilty like an animal caught feasting on something forbidden. Susan shut off the music, unplugged the baby monitor from the wall, and slipped out of the bonus room, carefully pulling the door shut behind her.

Alex was at the front door. "I'm so sorry. I forgot my keys," he said, then paused. "Honey? Are you OK?"

"Why?" she asked. "What?"

"What do you mean, what? You're naked. You're covered in paint. That is paint, right?"

Susan looked down. She was streaked and splattered, bright jagged lines of reds and blacks crisscrossing her chest and torso.

"Also, it's two in the morning."

"What?"

Two? That couldn't be right. She hadn't been in that little room for *five hours*, had she? "I was just doing some painting, is all. I got really into it." Susan's own voice sounded distant and unnatural. She felt exhausted; her muscles ached and her head swam. "Really? It's two o'clock in the morning?"

"Yeah. I'm really sorry I'm so late," Alex said. "After the shoot was finally over, I ran into Anton on the way to the subway, and I bought him a beer. He and Blondie are on the outs again, apparently."

Susan nodded, blinked. How had it gotten to be two o'clock?

*

She was so tired she could barely make it up the stairs. But once she had brushed her teeth and peed and collapsed into bed, Susan couldn't sleep. Alex, of course, passed out easily and immediately, and she lay watching him for half an hour before slipping out from under the sheets. She considered taking an Ambien but decided it was too close to morning, and she was already pretty drunk on the wine. She went to the bathroom, peed again, and then washed her face and hands, watching as flecks of paint spiraled down the drain. On her way back to bed, she lifted Alex's jeans from where he'd shed them onto the bedroom floor and was halfway to the laundry hamper when she noticed a curious square bulge in the pocket. Susan hooked two fingers into the pocket and came out with a matchbook from the Mandarin Oriental Hotel.

Two in the morning, Susan thought immediately, and looked over at him in his easy slumber. *Hotel matches?*

It took her about five seconds to remember that the girl they called Blondie, the on-again-off-again girlfriend of Alex's college friend Anton, worked at the Mandarin Oriental as a concierge. She'd occasionally gotten them theater tickets, before they had Emma and could still occasionally leave the house at night. A warm wash of relief flooded Susan—Alex had used Anton's matches, and Anton had gotten them from Blondie, who worked at the Mandarin. *Hotel matches, indeed. Moping around like the wife in a country-western song . . .*

She slipped back under the covers, laughing uneasily at her own paranoia. *Jesus H. Christ*, she thought distantly, as sleepiness began to settle over her, *what is this place doing to you?*

It was very early in the morning on Saturday, September 18. Susan, Alex, and Emma Wendt had been living in Brooklyn Heights for six days.

9.

Five hours later, Susan opened her eyes and saw a single tiny spot of blood on her pillow.

Except it wasn't blood. Except maybe it was. The room was dark, she was half asleep, and Susan couldn't really tell. It looked like blood. She rolled over, blinked at the glowing red lines of the clock radio, and moaned softly: 6:36 a.m. A good twenty minutes before Emma's usual wake-up time, and there was no reason for Susan to have woken.

The spot on the pillowcase was a few inches from where her face had been, just below the line of her mouth; it might even have been a puddle of drool, but it was too small and too contained. A dark crescent-shaped speck, ragged at the edges, the size and rough shape of a chewed-off fingernail. Alex slept on, snoring and openmouthed. Susan propped herself on one elbow, listening to her breath, and peered at her pillow. Now the speck looked a deep muddy gray against the lemon yellow pillowcase; now, as dead orange glimmers of day crept under the shades, it resolved itself into a dull brownish red.

Oh, she thought. *It's paint. Duh.*

Susan flicked at the speck with the nail of her pointer finger, expecting it to come right off. But the speck stayed where it was, bled into the cloth of the pillowcase. Susan pressed at it gently with the pad of a fingertip, and the firm pillow gave way slightly under the weight of her push.

It's nothing. Just—it's nothing.

Susan let her head drop back to the pillow and closed her eyes to the dot. She willed herself back to sleep, knowing it was futile. At last, at 7:12, Emma began to fuss over the monitor, and Susan smiled, as always, at the sound of her daughter's sweet morning noises. The rustle of the sheets, the give of the springs as Emma shifted her weight on her thin IKEA mattress, the first purring, hushed, "Mama?"

Susan opened her eyes, thinking maybe the tiny spot would be gone, faded like a fragment of a dream. But it was still there.

*

Five minutes later, Susan was crouched beside the toilet while Emma peed. She heard Alex roll out of bed, followed by a series of rustling noises and *whomps* as he made the bed and tossed the throw pillows in place. Then the noises stopped.

"Hey, Sue?" he called. "Did you see this?"

Crap. If Alex had noticed the spot, even in the morning-dark of the room, even while making the bed in his inimitably hurried, that'll-do-just-fine style, then it must be larger and more distinct— more real—than she had hoped.

"Go ahead and flush, and wash your hands, Em."

In the bedroom, Alex had flicked on Susan's bedside reading light and angled its gooseneck over the pillow, haloing the lamp's sixty watts around the crescent-shaped stain.

"Is it paint?"

"Maybe. I have no idea."

Susan, for some reason, didn't let on that she had seen it before, that she had already eliminated the possibility of dried paint. Alex made a little "hmmm" and pushed his curly hair out of his eyes. "What about blood? I think it's blood."

Susan winced. *All right folks,* she thought. *Let's not get carried away.*

"Did something bite you?"

"No." Susan raised a hand to her neck, ran her palm searchingly along her cheek. "I don't think so."

"But it is blood? I'm right, right?"

"No. I mean, I don't know."

"What could have bitten you?"

"I seriously have no idea."

But the answer skittered across in the back of her throat, nasty and furtive: *Bedbugs, bedbugs, bedbugs.* She thought of the article about the co-op board. The news, in fact, had been overrun by bedbugs lately, stories of renters suing their landlords, shops emptied of customers, hotels shut down on busy weekends so teams of exterminators could flush out the infestations.

"I'm sure it's nothing," Susan said. "Maybe it is paint. It probably is, actually."

Alex crossed his arms and sighed. Emma had come in and was sitting at the foot of their bed, cross-legged in her nightgown with the owls and stars, tossing Mr. Boodle gently up and letting him fall into her lap like a parachutist.

"Is it even red?" Susan asked, squinting at the spot. "Look."

Alex squinted at it, too, then looked at her questioningly. "I mean, yeah. It is."

"You don't think it's more of a brown, kind of?"

"Well . . . "

They stood side by side, bent at the waist and peering at the pillow, like two doctors examining a patient's cracked-open ribcage.

"Yeah," said Alex finally. "Actually, you're right. I think it's just dirt."

"I'm not sure," Susan said. "Maybe it *is* blood."

"No way." Alex straightened up, certain. "It's dirt. Watch."

He chipped at the spot, held his thumbnail to the light, and seemed satisfied. But Susan couldn't see that anything had come off the pillowcase, nor that there was anything under his nail.

"Dirt," he pronounced with cheerful finality and clicked off the bedside light. "Phew. Now I can go to the bathroom." He stretched and patted Emma on the way to the door. "I mean, that's just what we need, right? Bedbugs."

"Seriously," Susan said lightly, but her eyes were still trained on the pillowcase; the stain was still there, maybe slightly fainter than it had been, but still defiantly *there*.

Bedbugs. She had the sudden and absurd idea that by saying the word aloud, that small skittering word Susan had been trying so hard not to say, nor even to think, Alex had invited them in. He'd given the dark spot permission to turn out to be blood, after all.

Susan scratched her neck. *Did* she feel a small itch?

"Mama? What's bedbugs?"

Emma had padded over and now stood on tiptoe at Susan's side, trying to see over the lip of the bed.

"Oh, honey. They're nothing."

"They're these itty-bitty buggies, Em," called Alex from the bathroom above the steady tinkle of his urine stream. "They're super small, and they live in beds and bite people. And drink their blood."

Emma looked up at her mother with alarm, and Susan scooped her up.

"But guess what?" she said. "We don't have them."

*

The day bloomed glorious, with sunlight pouring through the windows, a perfect late-September Saturday. Susan put on coffee and oatmeal, played They Might Be Giants on iTunes, and led Emma through their exuberantly silly "morning exercises" while Alex showered. Then, while the girls ate breakfast, Alex did his elaborate routine where he kept appearing in different states of undress: First in just shirt and underwear; then just pants and a baseball cap; then shirt, shorts, and swim fins; each time asking earnestly "*Now* am I ready to go out?" and sending Emma into fresh hysterics. Susan felt flooded with pleasure and gratitude: Here they were in their big apartment with two floors, with the wide, tree-lined street outside, just a happy family clowning around on a Saturday morning in Brooklyn Heights.

We did it, she thought, plopping Emma down on the hardwood of the living room and wriggling her tiny feet into their puppy slippers. *We're here.*

"Now," Alex said, spooning brown sugar into his oatmeal. "I was thinking. Why don't I take the ragamuffin to ballet, and then to the playground or whatever. You relax for the morning and meet us for lunch."

"Really? Are you sure?"

"Totally."

"Dada's going to take me?" Emma sang, pirouetting unevenly on the hardwood. "Dada's going to take me!"

"You've been working like a madwoman to get this place put together and then had to be on duty all day yesterday. Take a break."

"OK. I mean, I still need a couple things at the drugstore. And if the bank's open—"

"No. Sue. Chillax. I implore you."

As she showered, Susan laughed at herself for freaking out about the teensy smudge on her pillowcase. She located her overreaction in a lifelong pattern of jumping to the worst possible conclusions. In college, for example, she had been certain on two separate occasions that she'd contracted Lyme disease, based on the scantest possible symptomatology. In her twelfth week of carrying Emma, after binging on alarmist websites, she'd frantically announced to Alex that hers was an ectopic pregnancy—a fear that proved mercifully fantastical.

Susan smiled a goony smile at herself in the mirror as she combed her hair, darkened and wet from the shower. *The house is great,* she told herself. *The neighborhood is great. And I even did some painting last night.*

She dressed quickly, not bothering to glance again at the spot on her pillow.

*

Susan trotted down the interior steps and out the door of 56 Cranberry Street an hour and a half later in black flats and a simple blue cotton jersey dress—a perfect ensemble for meeting one's charming husband and daughter for lunch on Montague Street. Andrea Scharfstein was at the bottom of the front stoop, looking up at the big red front door, almost as if waiting for Susan to emerge. Her hands were planted on her hips, and she wore a wide-brimmed gardening hat, a flowing green housedress, and those crazy old-lady sunglasses Susan so admired.

"Good morning," called Susan, waving brightly as she came down the stairs.

"Hello, hello." Andrea squinted over the tops of the glasses. "Where's the family? Did they leave you and find some other mother?"

"No. They're out and about," said Susan, thinking, *strange joke.* "I'm on the way to meet them for lunch." She stopped at the bottom of the steps and turned to stand next to Andrea. "Whatcha looking at?"

"Oh, nothing. Nothing, really."

Andrea slipped one old, sticklike arm through the crook of Susan's arm and leaned her head against her shoulder, like they were best friends, or mother and daughter. The gesture, so intimate and unexpected, flustered Susan, but she recovered and brought her other hand across her midsection to pat Andrea on the forearm. Susan's mother had been struck and killed by a drunk driver, two years after Susan's college graduation. She had been on a hostel-hopping painting tour of Europe, having the time of her life, when she got the telephone call. She had cried for seven hours on a plane from Paris and signed up to take the LSAT three days after the funeral.

"I hope the apartment is OK," said Andrea throatily, then coughed twice and turned her face toward Susan's. "Is the apartment OK?"

There was a deep-set, unsettled melancholy under the growl in Andrea's voice, and a sort of confusion. For the first time Susan wondered if Andrea, for all her seeming vigor and spiritedness, wasn't beginning to slip into senility. The arm still linked in Susan's was old but it was sturdy, yellow and clustered with age spots. Halfway up the forearm was a small open sore, red and bright and glistening in the sun.

"The apartment is just fine, Andrea. Thank you. We love it."

"There's nothing I can do to make it better for you?" Andrea lifted her sunglasses and searched Susan's face. "I want so much for you and your family to be happy here."

It occurred to Susan that Andrea *wanted* her to throw out a couple of problems that she could solve, that her elderly landlady somehow craved the reassurance of being responsible for someone else's welfare. "She seems . . . oh, just sad, I guess," Louis had said. "The house has a whole lot of sadness in it."

"Well, OK," said Susan. "Actually, there are a couple of, you know, just a couple of little things." Quickly she ran down the short list of minor problems they'd discovered since moving in last week: the broken floorboard on the upstairs landing; the cracking paint in the downstairs bathroom; the loose outlet cover in the kitchen.

"Those aren't *little* things, Suze," said Andrea. "Not at all."

Suze? The nickname made Susan's skin crawl, but she said nothing. Andrea at last pulled her arm free from Susan's, the wrinkles around her eyes and on her forehead multiplying as she furrowed her brow. "It's an old house, as I told you. As I *warned* you, really. But of course, of *course*, I will get Louis to take a look at everything, just as soon as he can."

"Thanks." Susan paused, bit her lip. "I feel like there was one more thing."

"Yes?"

The word scurried across her throat again, nearly slipped out onto her tongue: *bedbugs. Bedbugs. Tell her about the—*

But of course she had decided there were no bedbugs—hadn't she?—and she could hardly complain to the landlady about a spot of dirt on her pillowcase. "Oh, right, I know. There's been this kind of noise. Like a . . . " She gestured vaguely with her hands. "Like a *ping*, kind of."

"A *ping*?" Andrea narrowed her eyes. She was now standing with one foot on the bottom step, and Susan noticed that she had come outside wearing a pair of thin-soled lime green slippers. "Where is it coming from?"

"Well, that's what's weird," Susan said, a little embarrassed even to have brought it up. "I'm not exactly sure. We've just sort of heard it, generally. Mostly in the living room area, I guess. It's extremely faint, and it never lasts for very long. Not a big deal, really."

"Don't worry," said Andrea. "I'll take care of it myself."

Somewhere out over the East River the sun drifted behind a bank of gray clouds, and 56 Cranberry Street was momentarily cast in shadow, silhouetted like a black crepe cutout hung on the backdrop of sky. It was almost noon, time for Susan to be at Theresa's with her man and child, eating a tuna sandwich and hearing funny stories about ballet class. As if sensing her impatience, Andrea abruptly began to hike up the stoop.

"Anyway, Suze," she said. "We'll speak another time." As Susan watched, Andrea pulled the big red door closed behind her.

*

The rest of the weekend unspooled in a series of happy, easy hours. After lunch on Montague Street, Susan, Alex, and Emma strolled the tree-lined streets, exploring their new neighborhood as a family. They stopped at the drugstore, at the bank, and at Area Toys to buy Emma a jigsaw puzzle. At the farmer's market on Cadman Plaza they bought a bag of ripe Honeycrisp apples, a thing of frozen sausage, and three bundles of asparagus. After nap, Susan and Emma did the jigsaw puzzle, Susan marveling as her precocious genius-child patiently sorted through the twenty-four oversized pieces to assemble the barnyard scene.

"I take it all back," Alex said that night as he fried the asparagus with olive oil and salt. "This kitchen is actually terrific." He winked at Susan and she winked back. When Emma was asleep they polished off a bottle of Prosecco and made love on the living room floor—their first time since moving to Brooklyn.

Sunday morning Susan walked over to the Laundromat with a load of whites, leafed through the *Times* magazine until the buzzer buzzed, and then switched the stuff over to the dryer. When she caught up with Alex and Emma at the playground, she smiled to see that they'd met up once again with Shawn, and that Shawn had a seven-year-old sister named Tarika, with a pair of braided pigtails and a gap-toothed smile. The two families ended up having lunch at the Park Diner, and by dessert Emma was head over heels for Tarika, trailing the girl faithfully to the cookie case and hanging on her every word like revelation.

"Oh, shoot," Susan said suddenly, hours later, as Alex and Susan lay in bed reading.

"Shoot what, gorgeous?"

"I gotta go back to the Laundromat. Our stuff is still sitting in the dryer."

"No way, dude." Alex tossed his *New Yorker* on the ground. "I'll grab it."

"You sure?"

"Am I sure?" He grinned and hopped out of bed. Susan smiled, feeling safe and sleepy. "What are husbands for?"

Alex tugged on his blue track pants, planted a loud kiss on her forehead, and was gone. For once, Susan drifted off easily and was still sleeping soundly twenty minutes later, when Alex came home, folded the laundry, and put it all away—including the pillowcase that had borne the small and curious stain.

10.

On Monday morning at 9:13, Susan stepped into the bonus room, cried out, and dropped her coffee cup. The ceramic mug smashed to pieces on the hardwood, splashing Susan's legs with scalding liquid where they peeked out from her pajama bottoms. She screamed again, in pain and surprise, stumbled backward and clutched the doorframe, but her eyes remained locked on the portrait. Though still half complete, it was nevertheless an excellent rendering, a vivid and precise re-creation of the girl in the photograph that she'd stuck on the lower-right-hand corner of the easel. Sweet, funny Jessica Spender with her slash of scarlet bangs, her wicked and amused expression, her high cheekbones and red lipstick.

Except *there*, along the left cheekbone, Susan had given the girl a row of nasty welts, three of them in a line, running at a slight angle from the far corner of the left eye down to the nostril. Three marks, three round, raised, red circles, each with a pinprick of white at its dead center. The marks were carefully executed, and Susan did not remember painting them at all.

Marks?

No. Bites.

She had given Jessica Spender a row of bites.

Bedbug bites, her mind hissed. *They're bedbug bites, they're totally—*

Susan slammed the door and retreated into the living room, her hand pressed to her chest. She bit her lip and pressed the heel of her palm into her eyes, trying to summon memories of Friday night, her intense hours of painting, her ... binge? Trance? Whatever state of hyperfocused semiconsciousness she had entered into. The rest of the painting was carefully realistic, taken directly from the photograph. Except she had decided, some part of her had decided, to add the marks. The bites.

Could she have done that kind of work, that kind of careful work, without remembering it? And why would she?

Susan thought of the blood on her pillow—*paint, paint, I thought we decided it was paint? Or dirt, a smudge of dirt? What did we say?*—and a wrenching shudder traveled down her spine.

"Hey, Sue?"

Marni was hollering from the kitchen, where she'd been busily gathering snacks and plastic utensils, getting Emma ready for departure. "We're taking off, if that's OK?" The nanny was being extra solicitous, trying to make up for her supposed illness on Friday, which had miraculously resolved itself in time for a concert Saturday night at Hammerstein Ballroom.

"Wait," said Susan, and hurried down the hall. "One second."

"Hi, Mama." Emma was ready to go: she had on her shoes, her little jean jacket, her oversized Dora the Explorer backpack. Marni stood with the diaper bag slung over one shoulder, the strap running snugly between her breasts.

"Emma, honey," Susan said, "Mommy needs to ask you something."

In the bonus room she guided Emma carefully around the broken shards of the coffee cup and stood her before the easel. Susan gave her daughter's hand a reassuring squeeze; at nearly four years old, she could sense when her mother was upset about something, and to worry that she was the source.

"Emma, do you see these little dots on the woman's face?" she asked gently. Emma raised herself up on her tiptoes and nodded gravely. "Honey, did you make those dots?"

Emma shook her head vigorously, her bangs flopping on her forehead.

"Are you sure? Maybe on Saturday, before dinner? When Mama and Dada were in the kitchen? You were playing by yourself in the living room, did you maybe . . . ?"

But Emma kept shaking her head, her tiny brow creased with adamance. "No, Mama. I *didn't*."

Susan felt a presence and glanced up. Marni was hovering in the doorway, head tilted to one side, scrutinizing the portrait of Jessica Spender. Susan cast her an irritated look, and she backed away.

"Mommy's not mad, honey. I just need you to tell me the truth. Did you touch my painting?"

Suddenly, urgently, Emma threw her arms around her and buried her face in Susan's neck, breathing hotly into her throat.

"Can we leave, Mama? I don't *like* this room."

"Sure, Em, just—"

"I don't *like* it!"

*

Susan cleaned the spilled coffee and the broken mug, gathering up the shards into a paper bag and mopping the floor on hands and knees with a wad of paper towels. Down here on her knees, she could

still smell it, even under the rich bitter smell of the coffee: that abandoned cat, its dying reek of piss and rot. The painting stood on its
easel above her, still and silent. The truth was, Emma couldn't have
messed with it, even if she'd gotten it in her head to do so. She would
have had to drag in the stepstool, drag it back when she was finished,
not to mention mix the colors and clean the brushes and. . . .

I did it. I painted that picture that way, and I don't know why.

Susan felt a darkness welling in her veins. She rose from her
cleaning crouch and stepped to the painting, ran her hands over the
three dots marring Jessica Spender's beautiful cheeks.

I'm sorry, Jessica, she thought, as if she'd vandalized not the painting but the girl herself. *I'm sorry.*

*

Twenty minutes later, Susan was out the door and on her way to
the Brooklyn Heights Promenade. She would, she had decided, sit
with her sketchpad and charcoal pencils, watch the stream of joggers
and the middle-aged Caribbean nannies pushing their strollers; she
would set her artist's gaze on the Manhattan horizon and sketch the
magical skyline. She hustled down Cranberry Street, feeling the September sun on her cheeks. Turning right onto the Promenade, she
dug her iPhone out of her coat pocket and called Alex.

"Hey, hon," he said tersely. "What's up?"

She could picture him, staring like an X-ray technician at his
computer screen, running the pixelated magnifying glass over an en-
larged JPEG of a diamond, searching out its flaws.

"Nothing, just a random question for you. Did you by any
chance do something to my painting?"

"Did I what?" She heard his fingers rattling over the keys.

"My painting, Al, the painting I'm working on in the bonus room."

"I'm sorry, Susan, could you hold on for just one sec?"

"Sure."

She was halfway down the Promenade now, and she tossed her bag onto a bench and sat beside it, looking out at the Statue of Liberty and Governor's Island. A few feet away, a knot of tourists was posing at the railing, framed by the view, leaning on one another and laughingly hoisting an Italian flag.

"OK. Sorry, babe. What is it again?"

"I—*careful!*" One of the tourists was bobbling a toddler up on his shoulders, and Susan had a lurching sensation of the boy tumbling over the railing, down into the rushing traffic of the Brooklyn-Queens Expressway below.

"Susan?"

The boy was fine. His father had his legs gripped tightly, one in each hand. Susan closed her eyes and opened them again, resumed breathing.

"When you got home on Friday night, I was working on a painting. In my . . . in that little room, behind the living room. Did you, by any chance, do something to it? Over the weekend?"

"Did I *do* something to it? Yes, dear. I baked it in a pie."

"Alex."

"I have not stepped foot in that room since we moved to Brooklyn." She heard rapid tapping: he was sending e-mails while they talked. "I seriously don't even know what the room looks like."

"Huh. It's the weirdest thing . . . "

"Susan? I am so busy today. Can we—"

"Yes. Of course. Get back to work."

Susan held her sketchbook in her lap for half an hour, staring out across the river.

*

When Alex came home that night, it was as if the easygoing, eager-to-please doofus with whom she and Emma had spent their weekend had been kidnapped and replaced with his sullen, irritable twin. He barely said hi, barely acknowledged the painted pinecone Emma had spent all afternoon making for him.

"You don't seem up for dinner," Susan said, trying to get a read on him. "Should I do grilled cheese?"

"Sure. Fine."

While Susan dug around to find the cheese for their sandwiches, he reached over her head and helped himself to a beer.

"Want to hear some great news? There was some old dude hanging out on our stoop just now, perched on the front step, smoking a cigar. I said, 'Excuse me?' as in, 'Can I help you?' but he didn't say anything. He just shifted over and gave me this big, extra-polite grin. Like he was doing me some big favor, you know, letting me into my own house."

Alex stalked over to the front window, pulling on his beer, and glared outside.

"If he's still out there in ten minutes, I'm calling the cops."

Susan was slicing cheese on the cutting board. "That's just Louis," she said.

"Louis? Who the hell is Louis?"

Alex's voice was too loud. Susan stopped slicing. Emma, at the kitchen table, looked up from her coloring book and back down again quickly.

"Remember, when Andrea told us she had a guy who did stuff around the place for her, like unclog the toilets and stuff? That's him."

Alex rolled his eyes, let out a derisive snort. "You have got to be fucking kidding me." Susan gave him a look—*language*—but he ignored her. "What is he, a thousand years old?"

Susan shrugged, heard herself parroting Andrea. "He doesn't look like much, but he gets the job done. Seriously." Alex sipped his beer and grunted. "So what's going on? How's work?"

"You don't want to know."

But he told her anyway. From all appearances, their hard work the previous week on the Cartier shoot had been for naught. Richard Hastie, the potential rep, was using the watch-face snafu as an excuse to pass them over on the Cartier contract in favor of a large Diamond District outfit called Stone Work.

"It's just classic. They've got more experience, he says, so Cartier feels more comfortable with them, but of course we can't *get* more experience without a big-time client. So we're stuck with the penny-ante stuff, and I'm spending half my time writing invoices and payment reminders, instead of taking pictures." He snorted. "At least when I'm taking a particularly stylish picture of a ring, I can *tell* myself I'm a real photographer.*"

"I'm sorry, honey."

Susan made the right sympathetic noises, but beneath the surface her anxiety blossomed to bright and busy life. She could hear every word that Alex was thinking but not saying: *This is all your fault, Susan. All your fault.* He was struggling, handcuffed to a sinking business, stripped of his artistic identity, and she got to stay home and make art?

Or sit uselessly on the Promenade and people watch, not making art at all?

"Come on, Susan, don't use the santoku knife to cut tomatoes."

"What?"

"We have a cheap tomato knife. Use that. I've told you, save the good knives for when you really need a good knife."

Emma went to bed early that night, and Alex and Susan watched *Hell's Kitchen* in silence. If Alex remembered her odd phone call, questioning him about her painting in the bonus room, he didn't mention it. Given his mood, Susan saw little point in reminding him.

11.

The next day, Susan made no effort to paint. Once Alex had left for work and Marni had arrived and taken Emma to a 9:30 story time, she walked, with her umbrella open against a damp and drizzly autumn morning, to a Court Street coffee shop called Cafe Pedlar. She ordered a cappuccino and a pretzel roll, settled at a table in a back corner, and contemplated the recent unsettling events.

By now, she had abandoned the idea that Emma or anyone else had snuck into the bonus room and messed around with her work. She had painted the marks—*bites, the bites, the bites*—but could not for the life of her imagine why. Did this strange act of automatic painting represent the emergence of some cache of artistic energy lurking in her subconscious? Was she, in fact, an artist of exceptional brilliance, whose talent lay buried beneath calcified layers of ego and superego?

"No," she said aloud, and snorted derisively. "Probably not." A bearded dude in a Bob Dylan T-shirt, sitting with an iPad at the next table, glanced up and scowled. Susan smiled apologetically.

So, what, then? Had a ghost painted the row of red bites? A poltergeist?

She shook her head, sipped her coffee. Susan had never had much use for the supernatural, or even the religious. At her mother's

funeral, she'd knelt by the open casket, said the required words, thinking the whole time how stupid it all was. This was not her *mother* laid
out before her, this was a broken machine, a dead thing, ready to be
lowered back into the earth from whence it came.

Susan sighed. Probably she was just a lunatic. She remembered an
article from the *Times* magazine section, from a few years ago, about
people who do bizarre and unaccountable things in their sleep: punch
their spouses, eat raw steak, urinate on the floor. She'd sleepwalked down
the stairs in the middle of the night, Friday night, or maybe it was Saturday, added the dots to the painting, and slipped back into bed.

That had to be it.

The other thing that kept playing in her head was a vision of
Louis, standing in the newly cleaned bonus room with his hands
knotted together anxiously: "This house has always had sort of an *atmosphere* to it. Something. And well, there's a whole lot of sadness in
the place, since Howard died."

. . . a whole lot of sadness in the place . . .

Oh, would you stop it, Susan told herself. The Bob Dylan guy
scowled at her again. Susan smiled very politely, gave him the finger,
and got up to leave.

*

On the way home, Susan stopped at Dashing Diva on Smith
Street for a manicure, pedicure, and waxing.

"You bite your nails, ah?" said the manicurist, a small Korean
woman named Lee with a tall pile of shellacked black hair and a
frozen smile.

"What? Oh, years ago."

Susan had developed the habit in the months after her mother died and cured herself only years later, with a combination of hypnosis and the gross pepper-spray-type stuff parents smear on the nails of their thumb-sucking children. But now Lee's plastic smile flickered with confusion, and when Susan looked down she saw that her nails were raw and ragged, with red spots at the corners where she had chewed away the skin.

*

That night the family ate in silence. After Emma was in bed, Alex did the dishes, complaining several times about the "bucket of crap" under the sink. Susan had dutifully been tossing vegetable matter under there, periodically running the plastic containers down to the foot of the steps for Andrea to compost. When he was done with the dishes, Alex turned on his laptop and sat on the sofa, his glasses pushed up into his hair, his palm pressed to his forehead. Susan puttered around, sending out small feelers—"Do you mind if I put on some music?" "I thought we'd try that place Jack the Horse this weekend, if we can get Marni on Saturday night"—and earning only caveman monosyllables in return. Once she glanced at the screen and was surprised to see not a photograph of a diamond or a watch, blown up to full-screen view so Alex could scour it for flaws. Instead, there was a long column of figures, which he was scrolling through, jotting notes on a yellow pad beside him and muttering.

"Honey?" she ventured at last, knowing she was being nosy and annoying but unable to help herself. If the company was in financial trouble, if *he* was in financial trouble, then she was, too. "Whatcha looking at?"

"The books," Alex said curtly.

"Of the company?"

"Yes." Alex snapped the computer shut and stared at her challengingly. "Of the company."

"And—"

"Don't really feel up to chatting about it, OK?"

Susan tensed, flew up her hands, and retreated. This kind of outburst was so unlike Alex, and it confirmed exactly what she'd been thinking all that day: something was wrong around here, something had . . . had *darkened* somehow. It was more than just a few red dots on a painting. It was like since moving to Cranberry Street, her family couldn't quite get their footing. Alex was tense and distracted; she was going on somnambulant painting sprees. And wasn't even Emma quieter than usual, more distant?

Or wasn't it more likely that she was imagining things, casting into the anxious waters of her mind, fishing for new things to worry about? Alex was having a rough patch at work, that was all. Hadn't this past weekend been nice? More than nice—it had been perfect.

Things would revolve back to normal, to happy, as they always did. They had their problems—had had them in the Union Square apartment, too—but happy was the default setting.

Susan went upstairs, brushed her teeth, took a whole Ambien, and lay in bed thinking *mistake mistake mistake, I made a terrible mistake.*

*

The bedside clock read 1:12 a.m. when Susan gave up on sleep and went downstairs. In the kitchen she poured herself a tall glass of red wine, drank half in a long swallow, and then refilled it to the brim.

Clutching the wineglass in one hand, she walked through the living room in the darkness, drawing up her bathrobe against an unsettling sensation of eyes peering at her from the corners of the room: hundreds of eyes, thousands of them, staring at her. Living things tracking her hesitant steps in the darkness.

Slowly, with dread uncoiling itself in her stomach, Susan pulled open the door to the bonus room and then let out a low, shuddering moan. There was just enough moonlight to see the half-finished portrait of Jessica Spender, and it was covered in bites. Dozens and dozens of the nasty red spots, clustered in groups of three: three on the neck, three above and three below the eyes, two groups of three along the ridge of the nose, more circling the chin and cheeks.

Susan barely made it to the kitchen in time to retch, emptying the contents of her stomach violently and painfully into the sink, thick wine-stained vomit choking up into her throat. She coughed and gagged, loudly, hoping to hear Alex's groggy voice from the top of the stairs, calling down with hushed nighttime kindness, asking her if she was all right.

But the house radiated silence. Susan drank three glasses of water in the empty kitchen and went back upstairs to try again for sleep.

*

When Emma began to chirp over the monitor on Wednesday morning, Susan had slept for two hours, three at the most. She stumbled through the morning routine with a cup of strong coffee and a dazed expression. Alex declined breakfast and hurried out, unsmiling, at 7:25; an hour and a half later, Emma was gone, too, on her way down the steps with Marni, crying bitterly that she didn't want to leave mommy, a performance she hadn't put on in many months.

Susan settled heavily into a kitchen chair, ran a hand through her greasy hair, and laid her palms flat on the table. "Let's get some shit *done*," she told herself. "Forget all this haunted-house BS and get some shit *done*." There was a friend of hers from college, Kerry Feigue, who talked like that: brash, hyperconfident, unapologetic. Susan liked to conjure up an internal version of Kerry at times like this, when she could use a swift internal kick in the pants. She opened her MacBook at the kitchen table and let her hands hover over the keys. Alex had asked her, a few days ago, to order a new nonstick frying pan to replace one scratched in the move; she could go to Amazon.com, read customer reviews for ten minutes, and buy one. She'd also been meaning to follow up on the first couple suggestions that Vanessa, Shawn's mom, had given her for local preschools.

Instead, she Googled "bedbugs" and clicked on the first search result, a site called BedbugDemolition.com. The site was chaotic and unstructured, with one page titled "Sleep Tight," one called "Ask the (Sort of) Expert," and one just called "Pictures! Pictures! Pictures!" The webpage was amateurish in its design, studded with arbitrarily bolded paragraphs and bristling with blinking pop-up ads for exterminators and cleaning services.

Susan clicked, almost at random, on a link that said "Everything You've Always Wanted to Know about Bedbugs But Were Afraid to Ask" and quickly scanned the bulleted list, which looked like it'd been written by a hyperactive elementary school student doing a report: "Bedbugs are *parasites*, which means they live off the blood of a host—that's you!" "Every bedbug begins life as a 'stage one' and molts its exoskeleton *five times* before achieving full maturity as a 'stage five'!" "Bedbugs can live *for more than a year* between feedings!"

"Great," Susan muttered. A couple more clicks, and she was engrossed in a fierce debate, ranging over many posts, about whether bedbugs bore a detectable odor: some people were saying no; others were saying that a colony smelled faintly of lemon or lemon-scented candles. One person argued passionately that bedbugs smelled of raspberries and cilantro, a smell that "gets much stronger before/during blood meals!"

Susan went back to the previous page, found the link that boasted "Pictures! Pictures! Pictures!" and clicked on it. She began to scroll down and immediately stopped—the first picture, posted by someone identifying themselves only as "0-684-84328-5@gmail.com," featured a row of three bites, each one red and raised, with a white dot in the center.

"Oh, crap," said Susan. "Oh, *crap.*" She reached up and scratched idly at the top of her left cheekbone, just below her eye. Then she clicked the tab for Google on her bookmarks bar and did a search for "Jessica Spender."

It was, at it turned out, a fairly common name. There was a Jessica Spender in Joliet, Illinois, who owned a pastry shop, but the picture showed a heavy middle-aged lady in a ruffled apron. Another Jessica Spender was in Detroit, quoted three times in a *Free Press* article about the ongoing struggle to rebeautify that city's beleaguered downtown. This Jessica Spender was twenty-seven years old, which sounded like the right age, but she was a lifelong resident of Detroit, not to mention black. There was a seventeen-year-old Jessica Spender in a high school in South Bend, a newborn Jessica Spender in a Babble article about jaundice, and on and on and on.

Susan tapped her chin and then tried "Jessie Spender" instead. This time, the first result was a Facebook page for someone named

Jess Spender—and this lead, at last, seemed promising. It listed no age or occupation, and the profile picture wasn't a picture of a person at all—it was an odd-angle photograph of the Williamsburg Clock Tower, with a big handlebar mustache Photoshopped over it. A very cutesie-clever, very Brooklyn kind of profile picture.

This is her, Susan thought.

They had no Facebook friends in common, but Jess Spender's account was set to allow incoming messages from anyone. *Even*, Susan thought with an uneasy snort of laughter, *people living in your old house, who have created a likeness of you and then covered it with some kind of biblical plague.*

She clicked the button that said "Send Jess a message" and typed quickly in all lowercase letters: "hi. if this is the jessica spender that used to live on cranberry street in brooklyn, i have a"

Susan paused, cracked her knuckles. She was going to write "a quick question for you," but she didn't exactly know what her question was.

What about "how's your face?" That's a pretty quick question, right?

Susan deleted "i have a" and instead wrote "there's a piece of mail here for you and it looks important. landlady does not have forwarding address." She signed with her name, her e-mail address, and then, after a brief hesitation, added her cell number as well.

12.

"Sue, I have been the worst friend in the world! Do you want to have lunch today? Can you come to the city?"

It was Friday morning when Susan's friend Jenna called with the last-minute invitation, and Susan accepted it eagerly. The week had passed in a blur: Each morning Alex grunted some muffled facsimile of "good morning" and left, messenger bag slung over his arm, travel mug of coffee in a one-handed death grip. Marni came and whisked Emma away, leaving Susan alone in the house, melancholy and uneasy, too freaked out by the bonus room to do any painting, or much of anything else.

"Can we go somewhere with wine?"

"You bet your sweet ass we can!"

Jenna was an actress, the rare kind who actually made a living, performing frequently Off Broadway, occasionally *on* Broadway, and the rest of the time doing TV commercials and voice-overs. She was nice to a fault, a habitual self-deprecator, constantly pooh-poohing her substantial accomplishments and professing astonishment at Susan's life—at her *perfect* child, at her *gorgeous* husband.

Susan spent the morning in a better mood than she'd felt in days, enjoying a brisk walk to the Gristedes on Henry Street to get flowers for the kitchen table and then taking her time in her closet, selecting the right outfit for lunch. She looked forward to hearing about Jenna's latest adventures and to sharing with a sympathetic old friend both her excitement and her misgivings about the house on Cranberry Street. Jenna, she knew, would make her see how silly she was being, how *lucky* she was with her *amazing* family and their *incredible* new apartment.

Susan left the house at 12:30 to meet Jenna at Les Halles at 1:15. The closest A/C station, on High Street, was out of service, so she doubled back toward the stop on Jay Street. This detour took Susan down Livingston, where she walked quickly past the improvised shrine to the Phelps twins: the small forest of white and pink roses, the clutch of woeful wide-eyed teddy bears.

*

"Oh my God, how *is* everyone? How's Emma?"

"She's great, she's really great. Here . . . "

Susan found the latest pictures on her iPhone, and Jenna leaned across the table to clutch her arm, gasping loudly at each shot. "No! Too cute! *Too* cute! God, Sue, what an incredible creature she is! I'm serious, I am so in awe of you."

"Of me? Come on. What about you? Fran sent me the article from *Variety*, by the way. About the Lillian Hellman festival."

Jenna waved her hands to dismiss any talk of herself and her own accomplishments. "How's Alex?

"Oh . . . " Susan exhaled, took a sip of her Merlot. "He's fine. Busy."

"Good, good. Busy is good, right?"

"Yeah."

There was a long pause. Susan bit her lip, ran a hand through her hair, and looked at her friend; Jenna returned the gaze with wide, empathetic eyes. "God," Susan said, laughing quietly. "I must look like hell."

"You look *beautiful*, Susan." Jenna reached across the table and took her hands. Susan and Jenna had been friends for about twelve years, since both dated a guy named William Vasouvian. They'd run into each other at DBA one night, after both were through with him, and bonded over draft beers and stories of what a moron William Vasouvian had turned out to be.

"What's going on, Suzaroo?"

Susan opened her mouth, then shut it again, smiled, shrugged. It was all so ridiculous. *Gee willikers! I think my paintbrush is possessed, Jenna! What do I do?*

"Not a big deal," Susan said instead. "Nothing. I think we might have bedbugs."

Jenna let go of her hands.

"You have to move." Jenna stared at Susan with an intense, unflinching expression. "I'm serious."

A prickly shiver ran through Susan, from the base of her neck to the small of her back; the way Jenna was reacting, it was as if she *had* said her house was haunted, or confessed that she was painting dark visions from the Other Side. She forced herself to laugh lightly and raised an arch eyebrow in reply. "Jenna, take it easy. I said we might have them. We probably don't. Besides—"

"So why did you say that?"

"Because I . . . oh, I don't know. There was this spot on my pillow, and I thought . . . " She had a powerful memory, of walking through the living room in the silence and darkness, of *being watched*. She almost said it, almost said, "I felt them watching me," but then didn't.

"Thought what?" Jenna said. "Have you been bitten?"

"No, Jenna. No."

But Jenna was shaking her head emphatically. "You have got to move. Get out of there. I'll help you pack."

"Jenna. Stop. You're freaking me out."

"Well, I'm sorry, but you *should* be freaked out."

The waiter set down two green salads with grilled chicken and a basket of bread. "Enjoy, ladies."

Jenna kept her eyes locked on Susan. "I mean, you've seen the news, right? These things are *everywhere*. I don't know what it's like in Brooklyn, but I have heard so many horror stories. People end up throwing away all their stuff, sleeping on the ground, moving a million times."

"Jenna."

"I knew this girl, Katie Wilkes, she was in *The Weir* with me, she was *engaged* to this guy, and then they got bedbugs, from a second-hand futon, she thinks. Anyway, it caused this huge strain between them. Whole thing fell apart." Jenna shook her head gravely and stabbed at her salad. Her BlackBerry vibrated on the table; she glanced at it but didn't answer. Susan wondered fleetingly who was calling Jenna and felt a stab of nostalgia for work, for assignments and deadlines and pay stubs and things to do.

"OK, Jenna. Thank you. But seriously, like I said, I don't think it's bedbugs."

Jenna took a bite of her salad. "What does Alex say?"

Susan took a bite of hers. "He doesn't think so, either."

Jenna sighed, picked up her BlackBerry, and began to scroll through it. "I'm going to give you this number. For this woman named Dana Kaufmann. She's an exterminator. Pest control, whatever they call it."

"Jenna."

"My friend Ron, who works at Actor's Equity, he made every-one put this number in their phones after they found bedbugs back-stage at the ATA. Apparently this lady is, like, the exterminator to the stars. She sprayed Maggie Gyllenhaal and Peter Sarsgaard's house, in Park Slope."

"OK."

"Will you call her?"

"If I need to."

Jenna let the subject drop, and they passed the rest of the meal more pleasantly, catching up on mutual friends and books each had recently read. Jenna said she would come out for a visit soon, and Susan promised to see the show she'd just started rehearsing, a new musical by Tom Kitt, one of the guys who wrote *Next to Normal*. Jenna said what she always said, which was, "Oh, you don't have to do that. You're so *busy* . . . "

When they were hugging goodbye, Jenna clutched her tighter than usual and then drew back and looked her in the eyes.

"Oh, and *perfect* little Emma," she said, her voice an urgent whis-per. "I'm serious, Sue. If it *is* bedbugs, you have *got* to move!"

*

Susan took the 2 train back, so she could avoid the creepy shrine on Livingston Street. When she got home it was 1:45 in the after-noon; Emma would be upstairs, already napping, and Marni would be inside, sprawled on the sofa, reading or taking a nap of her own. Susan stood outside the house with her hands on her hips, staring up at the dark shape of the house against the sky, in just the posture she had discovered Andrea in the other day. When she was about to climb the steps to go inside, the red front door swung open, and Louis emerged at the top of the stoop, whistling lightly and carrying a hammer in one hand. When he saw her, he stopped and squinted, as if taking a moment to remember who she was, before calling out a greeting.

"Well, hello there, Susan. How ya doin'?"

As he trotted down the stoop toward her, Susan stayed put, glancing at the little door beneath the steps.

"Louis, can I ask you a question?"

The old man stopped at the bottom of the steps and smiled. "Sure thing."

"Has Andrea ever had bedbugs?"

Louis came down the last step, and they were both on the sidewalk now, at the foot of the stoop. He leaned his bulk against the short wrought-iron fence and scratched his big bald head.

"No. No, I don't believe she has," he said slowly. "Not that I know of, anyway And if anyone would know, it's me."

"And what about the previous tenants. Jessica Spender, and whatever his name."

"Jack. That fella's name was Jack Barnum. I remember it, because it's like the circus, you know. Barnum. My kids always loved the circus. When they were little we used to take 'em to the Midtown Tunnel in the middle of the night, to watch 'em bring the elephants across. You ever do that?"

"No. But, Louis—Jessica and Jack, did *they* have bedbugs?"

"Nope. Boy, those kids didn't need 'em, though. They had plenty of other problems." Louis shifted his weight, bobbled the hammer in his palm. "Why you asking all this? You think you might have a problem?"

"No. No, I'm just—you know, it's in the news and all."

"Sure."

They stood in silence for a minute, and then Louis nodded and stood up. "All right. You take care now."

He began to amble down the street, but Susan wasn't ready to go inside.

"Louis?"

He stopped on the sidewalk and turned back toward her; cheerful still, happy to help, but puzzled, maybe just the slightest bit put out. A man ready to proceed with his day.

"Yes?"

I should ask him to fix the broken floorboard, Susan thought. *And the faucet, and the light-switch cover.* When she gave Andrea her inventory of complaints last weekend, the landlady hadn't written any of it down, and Susan suddenly felt sure she'd never actually mentioned it to Louis.

Instead she found herself asking, "What's in the basement, Louis?"

Louis's gaze hardened. "Look, now. I already apologized for scaring your girl."

"I know. I'm just curious."

"Curious, huh?" He stared at her, taking her measure, and Susan thought he might just walk away. But then he shrugged and walked back over to where she was standing, spoke in a low, careful voice. "This is between you and me, understand?"

She nodded.

"Strictly between you and me. Now, like I said, Howard killed himself before his blood could kill him first. What I didn't tell you, what I didn't *want* to tell you, but since you're asking. . . . "

He leaned in, and Susan did, too; their foreheads were nearly touching. "He did it here in the house. Right down in the basement, real late one night."

"Jesus."

Louis straightened up and glanced over his shoulder at Andrea's dark first-floor window, before continuing in an urgent whisper. "This is all part of . . . part of why I'm a little concerned about Andrea, see. After it was over, you know, she never . . . never let anyone go down there and, you know, *tidy up.* I don't know if you've ever seen a gunshot wound to the head, what happens to the wall, the floor . . . "

Susan grimaced. She was feeling warm and tired, the wine from lunch catching up with her.

"Most I could do, after they came and took his body away, before she shooed me off, was put the damn hunting rifle back in its trunk. Figured at least get the thing out of sight, so it wasn't hanging around taunting her whenever she went down there for a roll of paper towels. Rest of the basement's just as it was on the day, so far as I know. Goddamn horror show, pardon my language."

"What do you mean, so far as you know? You never—"

Louis shook his head. "She won't let me down there. Because she knows if I do go down there, I'm gonna get down on my hands and knees and clean up what poor Howard did to himself. It just isn't right, leaving a scene like that. Like it's some kind of death museum."

"Jesus."

"Yeah. Now, look, Susan. We're keeping this between you and me? Understand?"

"Sure. Of course."

Louis was smiling again, but there was coldness behind his smile, and force. It was not a request.

13.

The thundercloud that had hung low and heavy all week over Susan and Alex's marriage erupted with ferocity on Sunday night, just after Alex came down from putting Emma to sleep. Though he'd already had two beers with dinner, Alex went straight to the fridge, opened a third, and drank half of it in one long swallow. Susan, at the kitchen table finishing her dinner of salad and sliced roast beef, looked up and said—simply, casually—"Thirsty?" It was the kind of little bantering tease that would normally earn a comical assent ("As a matter of fact I am!") or, at worst, a dismissive and weary, "Ha, ha." But Alex, sullen and discontented as he'd been for days, stared back at her, bottleneck gripped tightly in his fist, and said, "What? What's the problem?"

Susan pushed her chair away from the table. He was spoiling for a fight, and Susan, in her own dark and unsettled frame of mind, found herself itching to give him one.

"What's *my* problem? Come on, Al. Something's making you all pissy, but guess what? You share your life with another person. Two people, in fact."

He made a sour face. "You don't have to tell me that."

Susan's steak knife trembled slightly in her grip. "What the hell does *that* mean?"

"Nothing." He exhaled, turned his face away from her and gazed down into the sink. "I'm just anxious about money. I have to write the rent check, and it's going to be a tough one."

"Oh."

As soon as he softened, Susan relaxed, too. This was all she wanted, for Alex to open up, to share what was eating him, instead of moping around like a human black cloud. Now she could do what spouses did, say all the right things about how it was going to be OK, how they were a team, how they could figure it out together.

But just as she said "Alex . . . ," he turned back around and said the magic words: "Especially since you're not working right now. . . . "

"Oh, for God's sake," Susan said sharply, tossing the steak knife onto her plate with a clatter. Over the baby monitor, Emma made a discontented moan in her sleep.

"What?" said Alex, with obnoxiously exaggerated innocence.

"I am just so sick of hearing you say that."

"Why? You were the one who decided to stop working."

"It wasn't unilateral. We talked about it a thousand times."

"Exactly. You talked me into submission."

Susan's jaw dropped. She felt like she'd been punched in the stomach. "And, by the way," Alex continued, jabbing his finger at her, his nostrils flaring, "*You* were the one who decided that we needed to spend several thousand dollars to move. To move to a *more* expensive apartment . . . "

"OK, well, once again, I didn't decide anything by myself."

"Oh, come on."

"You agreed with me!"

"I went *along* with you."

Susan snorted. "*Please*."

Alex shook his head angrily. She could see him building steam, convincing himself of the accuracy of his own memory. She felt aware of how much bigger he was than her, of his thick torso and big arms. "No, I did, I went along with you. I knew it was a stupid idea, but I gave in. That's different from agreeing."

"That's not fair, Alex. It's not fair and you know it."

All the while an accusing voice was chattering in the back of Susan's mind, an insistent and taunting whisper: *he's right, he's right, of course he's right*. It was *Susan* who had dragged them from their cozy nest off Union Square, it was *Susan* who saddled them with this new burden, with this new apartment—*which, by the way*, she thought crazily, *is very possibly haunted and/or infested with—*

She shook her head violently, wrestled her mind back under her control.

"So your business is tanking?" His eyes widened, and she liked it; she liked to see that she'd wounded him. "So I'll get a job! I'll go to a firm. I'll be making three times as much as you by next week."

"Great. And then you'll be wandering around here whining, every night, how miserable you are . . . how hard things are for you . . . "

"Oh, like you've been doing for the last two weeks?"

The fight carried on for hours, the kind of interminable and miserable argument that would peter out into brutalized silence, then flare suddenly back to life, worse than before—another round of re-criminations and accusations, snorts of derision, unrelated grievances dragged out to be aired and re-aired. When they fought this way, Susan imagined them as two mad and vicious dogs, tearing at each other's throats, charged with pure animal hatred. Later, lying awake, her heart pounding and her chest trembling from the exertion, Susan thought that without question it was the worst fight in the history of their marriage, the worst since they had known each other.

Beside her, Alex lay sleeping peacefully, his flesh gently glowing in the moonlight, a line of spit running down his fleshy cheek. Like a child. Like nothing had happened. Susan stared at the cracks in the ceiling. She resisted the urge to shake him awake, scream in his face, go for another round. His easy slumber was just one more attack on her, one more way of making her feel bad.

Christ.

Every night, it seemed like there were more cracks in the goddamn ceiling.

*

The dream came again.

It began, this time, at the shrine on Livingston Street. She was sorting through the wilting pink roses and dirty teddy bears, trying to find a good one to take home for Emma. These bears had been out on this grimy street for so long, surely the fleas and maggots had had their way with them? But oh, Emma wanted one so, so Susan lifted the dilapidated toys one by one, looking into their dead black plastic eyes, running her hands through their matted fur. Until a throaty voice called *watch out*, and she looked up, up along the dizzying height of the building, and saw the massive double stroller tumbling down, faster and faster, spinning in the air, the twin girls screaming and screaming in their seats. The stroller slammed against the pole of the awning and hurled outward in a long final arc, sailing over Susan's head and bursting on the sidewalk beside her. Blood gushed out in all directions, great horrid fonts of blood, pouring down over her, running into her eyes and filling her mouth as she screamed and screamed—

—and woke, panting, with Alex shaking her. "Honey? Honey," he said, "It's all right." His eyes glowed with love and tenderness, and she collapsed into his bare chest, ran her hands desperately through his hair. He shushed her, cooed into her cheeks. "Your pillow is soaked," he said, and went to the linen closet to fetch a fresh pillowcase.

"No," she whispered, tried to whisper, but found the word lodged in her throat like a marble, round and hard. *NO.* He unfolded the pillowcase and flapped it once, neatly, and bugs went flying, like sand shakes out of a beach towel, thousands and thousands of bugs, their antennae twitching in the darkness, bugs coating the sheets and the floor. She could feel them, rushing in every direction, disappearing into every crack and corner of the room.

We'll never get them out—never get them out now. . . .

*

Her eyes shot open and she was awake this time, really awake. Quiet darkness. The ceiling. The cracks. It was 3:32 a.m.

The pillowcase, Susan thought. *The pillowcase!*

She slipped out of bed, her heart thudding *wham wham wham* in her chest, stepped out onto the landing, and opened the linen closet. The pillowcase, her pillowcase from last weekend, was still where Alex had tossed it indifferently atop the otherwise neat pile. She lifted the thin folded fabric under her arm and took it to the bathroom, where she shook it out and held it up to the vanity lights above the mirror. They had convinced themselves it wasn't blood, but it *was.* It was a small ragged circle of deep, rich red against the lemon yellow of the pillowcase.

It was blood.

Susan, in a sort of daze, carefully folded the pillowcase back up and laid it atop the pile. Then she stumbled back into the bedroom, collapsed into bed, and fell into a deep and dreamless sleep.

14.

The next morning Susan woke with three small bites on her arm. She stared at them, unsurprised. Three bites.

Susan flicked on the bedside light. Her bites were arranged in a neat row, just above the wrist. Each bite was raised and hard, the circumference of a dime, dotted with a white pinprick at dead center. For thirty long seconds, Susan looked at her bites.

Just like Jessica's, she thought, and then told herself to be quiet.

It was 6:42 a.m. on Monday, September 27. Susan and her family had been living in Brooklyn for fifteen days.

Emma was still sleeping, and she heard the water of Alex's shower through the wall. Susan flipped her pillow and ran her fingers over the case, holding the fabric closely to her eyes, but found no spots. Then she got out of bed, pulled down the comforter, examined the top sheet; she stripped it off and ran her hands along the length of the fitted sheet, from the top of the bed to the foot. Susan had a sense that this was what she had been waiting for; the floating unease she'd had in her gut for days now had been realized somehow, like a prophecy fulfilled.

The bites didn't hurt. She pushed at them with her fingertip, scratched gently at them, traced their outlines with one ragged fingernail. The water lurched off, and there was a pause, and then another stream, quieter; Alex was filling the sink to shave. Susan felt traces of anxiety and anger in her bloodstream, chemical traces of their horrid fight and her subsequent dream running in her blood like a hangover.

She walked to the door and flicked on the overhead, flooding the room with light, and carefully repeated her search. She ran her open palms first over her side of the bed, then his side. She remembered a desperate morning from a million years ago, her sophomore year of college, when she had woken beside a stranger, whom she had fucked—for some idiotic, unknowable, drunken reason—in her roommate's bed. After shooing the guy out, she had performed this same diligent, shame-tinged exercise, dreading the discovery, the flash of crimson, the incriminating stain.

The top sheet and comforter were piled in a heap on the floor, and Susan was on her hands and knees at the center of the bed, squinting at the fitted sheet like a bloodhound, when the bedroom door creaked open and Alex entered, wrapped in a towel.

"Susan?" he began. He was speaking softly, eyes on the floor, ready to do a postmortem on their fight. "So, look."

Susan shrieked. Above the thick nest of Alex's black chest hair was a trail of blood, bright red and dripping from his neck.

"Shaving," he said, raising his hand to the wound. "Must be worse than I thought."

Emma started to fuss over the monitor. "Mama?" she called out, half whispering, half singing. "Maaama?"

"Susan?" Alex crossed the room to stand beside the bed. "What . . . ?"

She shifted to a seated position and held her hands up to him, wrists extended, as if submitting to handcuffs. Alex saw the bites and let out a long, low whistle.

"Whoa. Looks like we need to call an exterminator."

*

You're in luck," said Dana Kaufmann, exterminator to the stars. "Ten o'clock today is available. Can you do ten o'clock today?"

Susan agreed readily, and Kaufmann arrived right on time, a butch, unsmiling woman in gray denim coveralls and baseball cap that read: GREATER BROOKLYN PEST CONTROL. She wore sturdy brown boots and carried a black duffel bag and a heavy flashlight, holstered in a loop of her coveralls. Susan felt better the moment that Kaufmann stepped into the apartment.

"Hi, good morning. Thank you so much for coming." Susan motioned to the kitchen. "Can I get you a glass of water or something?"

"No, thank you."

As they stepped into the sunlight of the kitchen, Kaufmann produced a thin spiral notebook from a pocket of her coveralls, cleared her throat, and clicked open a pen.

"Tell me about your bedbugs. What physical evidence have you had?"

"Just, uh . . . here." She pushed up her sleeve and showed Kaufmann the row of bites, feeling a quick tingle of embarrassment, like she was at the doctor, wriggling out of her underpants.

Kaufmann narrowed her eyes and muttered, "All right," as she appraised the marks. "And what about bugs? Have you observed any active bedbugs?"

"You mean—"

"By 'active,' I mean alive."

"No."

Kaufmann scrawled in her pad. "Inactive?"

Susan shivered. "No."

"Have you found any cast skins?"

"What would those look like?"

Kaufmann spoke rapidly, reciting a familiar passage. "Bedbugs molt five times between birth and maturity. Each time they shed their exoskeletons. Cast skins look like bugs, but empty and still and slightly transparent, measuring between a twelfth and a sixth of an inch."

"Oh."

Kaufmann paused for a moment, and then said: "So? Have you seen any?"

"Uh, no. Sorry. I haven't."

"Have you observed any bedbug larvae?

"What would—"

"Like little maggots. Or clear jelly beans."

Susan felt a wave of nausea, and she shook her head rapidly. "No, no. Nothing like that."

Kaufmann frowned and flipped to a fresh page in her notebook. "So what would you characterize as your main reason for requesting the services of a pest-management professional today?"

"Um . . ." *Well, you see, I'm having these nightmares, and there's this creepy painting, you see, Ms. Kaufmann, and* . . .

"It's the bites. Just the bites."

*

Dana Kaufmann began her search in the bedroom. She strode across Alex and Susan's ovular, modernist throw rug in her heavy boots and stripped the comforter and sheets from the bed in a quick, rough motion; Susan felt silly for having taken the time to make the bed after her feverish bug hunt that morning. Then, with a soft grunt, Kaufmann lifted the mattress and lay it at a steep angle against the wall. Like a security guard frisking a suspected terrorist, she ran her hands all around and across the mattress with deft efficiency, pushing in the surface with her palms, curling her fingers to run them along the edges. She produced a kind of long flat stick, like a nail file with pointed ends, and used it to probe the seams. Then, with another grunt, Kaufmann flipped up the box spring against another wall to perform the same thorough search, dancing her fingertips along the wood frame and gauzy stretched fabric.

Susan stood in the doorway, mesmerized.

At last Kaufmann cracked her knuckles, produced a small electric drill from an inner pocket of her coveralls, and inclined her head toward the black oaken headboard.

"You mind?"

"Um . . ."

"Don't worry, ma'am. I'll put it back."

The drill emitted a steady high-pitched whine as Kaufmann disassembled the headboard, slats, and legs of the bed, until Susan's precious low-slung Design Within Reach beauty was a neat stack of dark wood piled in the corner of the room. Kaufmann crouched by the pile and lifted up the various sections of the bed one at a time, turning each handsome piece of wood over in her hands. When she had satisfied herself with each constituent element she set it down on her other side. Susan wondered idly what kind of bed Maggie Gyllenhaal and Pete Sarsgaard had.

"You keep a lot of stuff under your bed," said Kaufmann, without turning her head.

"What? Oh, yeah. I guess." Susan looked at what had been revealed when Kaufmann took apart the bed: the neat line of shoeboxes and crates from Bed Bath & Beyond, shopping bags full of other bags, a couple rolls of wrapping paper, the case containing Alex's long-unplayed mandolin. "Is that a lot?"

"Bedbugs live in hidden spaces. They feed for ten or fifteen minutes and then, when they're sated from their blood meal, return to a dark safe space, close to the bed." Kaufmann jerked her thumb over her shoulder. "Shoeboxes? Clutter? Right under the bed? This is perfect, if you're a bedbug."

Susan nodded rapidly. "Right." She picked up a shoebox and took it toward the closet.

"Tell you the truth," said Kaufmann, still not looking up. "The closet's worse."

*

Dana Kaufmann put Susan's bed back together as promised, aligning the slats and drilling them back into the legs, reattaching the headboard with practiced ease. She slumped the box spring and mattress back in place but didn't go so far as to remake the bed. Kaufmann then slid the flashlight free of the loop where it rested and worked her way through the spacious bedroom closet, sweeping the powerful beam across in methodical rows, training it on the top and bottom corners one by one. To Susan's mind, the closet was neat and uncluttered; they had moved in only two weeks ago, so even Alex's deep-seated natural disorder had yet to take root. But Kaufmann exhaled disapprovingly over and over at each potential bedbug hideout she uncovered with the flashlight's beam: Alex's tangled forest of dress shirts; Susan's small fabric crate overspilling with tights and pantyhose; the high shelves above the clothes, stacked with sweaters in uneven piles.

Susan stood behind Kaufmann, arms folded across her chest, anxious sweat beading on her forehead. She kept waiting for the exterminator to beckon her over, to focus the beam beneath a sweater or inside a shoebox, to say, "There? See? There are your bugs."

But the minutes ticked by in silence, until Kaufmann at last turned off the light, gave her knuckles another crack, and said, "Let's move on."

Across the landing in Emma's room, Kaufmann disassembled and examined Emma's bed as swiftly and thoroughly as she had Susan and Alex's and then put it back together just as conscientiously. Kaufmann pawed through Emma's trunks and bags of playthings with her large hands, entirely uncharmed by the girl's helter-skelter universe of pink puppies and cockeyed dollies. She chased her fingers through the short fur of the stuffed animals like a monkey picking for nits; she opened the pages of picture books and shined her flashlight through the thin cotton of Emma's pajamas.

*

Kaufmann was down on her haunches in the kitchen, searching the cupboard beneath the sink, when a light rap sounded at the door.

"Suze?"

"Oh, hey, Andrea. Good morning."

"Oh, Susan, I am so sorry to bother you, but I was having this very odd problem with my computer, something about the, the network connection? I think? And I always see you going about with that laptop case, I wonder if . . . oh, dear—what's . . . what's this?"

Andrea's voice got high and flutey with anxiety. In her green house shoes and flowing silk pajamas that seemed from another century, she leaned through the front door, peering at Kaufmann. "Do we have some sort of infestation? Please say no."

"I'm not sure. We're looking. She's looking. We'll see."

"Well, I wish you had told me. I would've arranged for someone to come."

As Susan led Andrea into the kitchen, Kaufmann looked up and gave her a quick clinical glance, as if making sure she wasn't an enormous talking bug. "Of course, you'll take the cost of the exterminator off your rent. You haven't paid the rent yet, have you? No, I don't think you have."

"Thanks, Andrea."

Susan didn't offer coffee, but Andrea hung around anyway, hovering at Susan's arm in the kitchen doorway, watching as Kaufmann closed the cupboard and turned to the pantry.

"My sister, Nan, who lives in Portland—Portland, Oregon, not Portland, Maine—anyway, Nan once told me a foolproof system," Andrea said. "You're meant to sprinkle drops of liquor all over the house. I can't remember now what kind, of course. But I could call her. Shall I call her? According to Nan, sprinkling this, whatever it was, kills the bugs straightaway."

"Oh," said Susan. "Huh."

Kaufmann straightened up, clicked off her flashlight, and addressed Susan.

"If an apartment is infested with bedbugs, we employ a three-pronged solution. First a contact-kill solution; second, a liquid residual such as Permacide Concentrate; and third, a growth regulator such as Gentrol. If those solutions prove ineffective, there are various means of escalation available."

"Rum!" said Andrea, snapping her fingers. "If you sprinkle drops of rum in all the corners—"

"No." Kaufmann interrupted, scowling. "Do not do that."

*

Andrea left shortly thereafter, and Kaufmann requested a glass of water, which she drank in a single, long draft. "OK," she said when she was done. "Are there any areas of the apartment I haven't seen yet?"

As soon as they stepped into the bonus room, Kaufmann stopped.

The portrait of Jessica Spender was now covered in hundreds of bites; they lined the cheeks and chin and covered the forehead like stucco. Worse, Jessica's eyes had lost the teasing, insouciant expression they bore in the photo, and that Susan knew she had given them in her portrait: the eyes of the girl in the painting looked terrified, helpless, and pleading. A light gouache of tears had been laid over the pale blue of her irises.

Susan clapped a hand over her mouth and fought the urge be sick.

"That's really something," said Kaufmann, and turned to Susan with wondering eyes, a flicker of childlike awe peeking from behind her rock wall of professionalism.

"Yeah. I'm a—I'm a painter," Susan said inanely. She felt clammy; a row of sweat broke out across her brow; the room was spinning before her. Kaufmann continued staring at the painting, and Susan stared at it, too, against her will—she wanted to run desperately from that room, from the house, to take off down the street, find Emma, gather her up, and *go go go.*

"Well," said Kaufmann finally, and cleared her throat. "Not a lot of clutter in here. I'll be quick." She dropped to her hands and knees and began to crawl around the perimeter of the room, running her fingers along the baseboards. Susan stepped toward the painting, intending to take it down, roll it up, maybe even run it down the hallway and toss it into the kitchen garbage or, better yet, the stove.

Why did I do that to her? Susan demanded of herself. Her feet stayed frozen to the floorboards, her hands stuck at her sides. *Why?*

"Excuse me? Ma'am?" Kaufmann was talking. "Ms. Wendt?"

"Yes. I'm sorry. Yes?"

"What was in here?"

Susan pushed away a stray curl that had drifted in front of her eyes. "What?"

Kaufmann had paused in her perimeter crawl around the room, between the door and the left-hand wall. "These scratches just above the baseboards. Here. They're painted over, but you can feel 'em. Have you felt these scratches?"

"Uh, no. Actually, I hadn't." Susan didn't move. She didn't want to feel the scratches. What was the cat's name again? Oh, right. *Catastrophe.*

"There was a cat. It, uh, it died in here. Really sad."

"A cat, huh?"

"Yes." Susan felt the painting watching her, felt Jessica Spender's pleading, pitiful eyes. "Why?"

"Nothing. Forget it," said Kaufmann, straightening up. "Not my specialty. Anyway, I'm done. Let's talk in the kitchen."

*

As it turned out, there were no bedbugs in Susan and Alex's apartment.

Kaufmann had performed an exhaustive search, "from bow to stern," as she put it, and turned up no evidence of *Cimex lectularius,* or *Leptocimex boueti,* which—according to Kaufmann—would be even worse.

"Fortunately," she concluded, flipping closed her notebook. "You have neither."

"But . . . " Susan gestured vaguely to the notebook. "What about all those things you were saying. Contract kill, and, and residual—"

"Contact kill, ma'am."

"Please stop calling me ma'am. OK?" Susan was flustered. How could there be no bedbugs? It made no sense. "Call me Susan."

"That's fine, Susan. But listen, this is *good* news. Contact killers, residuals, control agents. These things are poisons, and you do not want your home treated with poison unless such a treatment is called for."

"But . . . "

"I found zero bugs, living or dead. I found no cast skins, no fecal matter, no larvae. I wouldn't say it's *impossible* that you have bedbugs, ma'am . . ." A smile flickered across Kaufmann's face. "*Susan*. But it's *impossible* that you have bedbugs."

"Wow." Susan forced herself to smile while her stomach twisted itself into greasy knots. "Well, I mean, that's great."

"Yes. It is."

"Wait, wait. What about my wrist?" She raised her hand, turned it wrist up, resisting the urge to hold it under Kaufmann's nose. "What about the bites?"

As she said it, the bites began to itch, as if she had reminded them of a neglected duty. She lowered her arm and tried to scratch non-chalantly while Kaufmann answered.

"Could be a lot of things. Scabies. Mosquitoes. Could be fleas, though I don't see any evidence of fleas. Do a Google search on spider beetles. Half the time, when someone's got bedbug bites but no bedbugs, what they've really got is spider beetles. I'm not a doctor, but I think you put some hydrocortisone cream on there, give it a week, and you'll be fine."

"OK. Thanks. Thanks so much."

"You're welcome." Kaufmann tucked her notebook back into her coveralls while Susan opened the door.

"It's two hundred for the visit. Tax free, if you've got cash."

*

"Oh, fantastic!" Alex enthused. "That's the best news I've heard all week."

"Yeah. I know."

Susan shifted the phone, jammed it under her chin, freeing her right hand to keep scratching at the welts on her wrist. The bites had continued to itch, and the scratching was barely helping.

"Listen, baby doll," Alex said. "I'm sorry I was such a jackass last night. Let's start over, OK? Remember that thing you read that time? How moving is, like, the most stressful thing that couples go through?"

"Right."

"Well, so, we moved. We're done. We've got a great new apartment, and there ain't no bugs in it. OK?"

"Yeah. Of course. Bye, babe."

"I love you, Susan."

She hung up and looked at her wrist. With all her scratching, the bites had opened into bleeding sores.

15.

Alex transferred money out of their "rainy-day" savings account to cover the rent. On Thursday night, September 30, he trotted downstairs, rapped on Andrea's door, and handed over the check. Susan stood on their landing, listening to the two of them chat.

"I stopped by the other morning," Andrea was saying in her gravelly undertone. "When the exterminator was here. Or does one say exterminatrix?"

Alex's big fake laugh bounced up the stairwell; Susan's husband was always a good one for laughing at other people's stupid jokes.

"Susan seemed quite upset, but I gather there's no infestation after all. That must be a relief to her."

"Oh, yeah," said Alex. "For me, too."

"Well, that makes three of us!"

Alex's laughter mingled with Andrea's throaty bray. Susan stood, listening, scratching at her bites. She had waited for them to fade, but they'd only gotten worse: the more she scratched, the more they bled and itched, and the more she scratched. She had taken to wearing thick bracelets every day, but when she was alone she slipped off the bracelets and attacked her wounds, moaning with relief. When she wasn't scratching she bit at her fingernails, digging her teeth into the flesh at the base of each nail. She had gotten used to the miniature teardrops of blood that would well up at the corners, and the tender swelling and mild pain that came after.

She had Googled spider beetles, per Dana Kaufmann's suggestion, and discovered in the all-knowing Wikipedia that they were beetles of the family Anobiidae, with "round bodies and long, slender legs." But the pictures of spider-beetle bites she found came in clusters of a dozen or more, not neat lines of three, and they were larger and redder than her bites had been. That's what Susan remembered, anyway; at this point, she had been scratching her wrist so relentlessly that the original bites were barely visible amid the subsequent self-inflicted damage. Meanwhile, Kaufmann's prediction was borne out: no new bites appeared, no new spots of blood appeared on the pillowcases, or anywhere else.

Alex's work, meanwhile, was turning around. Early October brought a raft of new clients for GemFlex, all of them small, but together enough to blunt the disappointment of having the potential rep slip through their fingers—what Alex now cheerfully called "The Hastie Incident."

Each morning, Susan carried her sketchbook to somewhere in Brooklyn. She went to the clock tower, she went to the Carousel in Prospect Park, she went to Fort Greene and sat in the shadow of the Martyrs' Monument. She did not return to the bonus room, explaining to Alex that she was finding oil painting unsatisfying and for now was experimenting with line drawing instead. He readily accepted this bland explanation, so Susan never had to reveal how terrified she was to go back into the little studio, to see in what state she would find her aborted portrait of Jessica Spender.

*

"Mama?" said Emma one afternoon, after waking up from nap. "I miss Shawn."

It took Susan a moment to remember who she was talking about. "Oh, sure, baby. Should I call Shawn's mama for a play date?"

Emma popped out of bed, grinning. "Yay," she said. "Shawn's coming over! Maybe Tarika will come, too! Do you think Tarika will come, too?" Susan laughed and squeezed Emma's leg—*sweet girl*. "I don't know. Let me call them first, hon."

She found Vanessa's number in her phone and then listened with a sinking heart while the other woman spoke in a cool, even tone. "Susan, this is really awkward, but are you guys having an insect problem?"

"What?"

"Shawn's coming over!" Emma was crowing, spinning in giddy circles around her room. "Tarika's coming over!"

"Emma, *please*," said Susan. "Sorry, Vanessa, what were you . . . "

"I'm really sorry. The kids and I were walking past your house the other day. We saw the exterminator coming down your stoop."

"Oh, God, Vanessa. No, no. We don't have bedbugs."

There was a pause. "Bedbugs?"

"We don't have anything."

Susan rubbed her forehead with her palm. She felt like she was going to cry.

"I'm sorry, Susan. I just can't risk coming over—the kids—"

"Of course."

She hung up and stared into space, the phone dangling in her hand while Emma spun around her, clapping. "Shawn's coming over! Shawn and Tarika are coming over!"

*

On Tuesday, October 17, Susan dialed the number for Greater Brooklyn Pest Management, not exactly sure what she intended to say. It's not like they had a spare two hundred bucks lying around for Kaufmann to come take a second look, even if she'd be willing to do so. When the exterminatrix answered with a gruff "Kaufmann," Susan panicked and hung up, like a kid making a prank call.

Instead, she called Jenna, and reached her at the Acorn, on Theatre Row, where she was in technical rehearsal for the Tom Kitt musical, which was titled *Dignity* and scheduled to open the following Tuesday.

"Susan, hey! I only have a second. How are you?"

"I'm fine. I'm OK. I wanted to let you know I called the exterminator you suggested. Kaufmann? The woman that your friend from Actors' Equity—"

"Oh, my God, so you *do* have bedbugs! *Susan!*"

"No. Actually, she came out, and she said we're clear."

"Well, *that's* good news. I'm sorry if I freaked you out."

"Yeah. Except—"

"Hold on." Susan could hear orchestra instruments in the background on Jenna's end: the muted bleat of trumpets, someone sawing at a double bass. "Sorry."

"That's OK. How's the show, Jenna?"

"It's wonderful. It's really great."

*

The last week in October, the *New York Times* ran a three-day series on the city's ongoing bedbug epidemic: one article on the lengths being taken by hotels to reassure worried customers; one on the devastation being wrought upon secondhand furniture and vintage clothing markets; one on the vogue for "bedbug-sniffing dogs," which were likely a scam, preying on the paranoid and anxious. Susan tried to ignore the articles, but Alex read the headlines aloud each morning: "There but for the grace of God, huh, gorgeous?"

The last days of late summer were gone now, and Susan was glad for the arrival of long-sleeve weather, the better to hide her gouged and inflamed wrist. Each night, after Alex went to bed, she swallowed an Ambien and stood at the foot of the bed for a long time, staring at the rough triangle of exposed sheet where she had pulled down the corner of the comforter. She would listen to Alex's soft, even breathing, then force herself to get in.

BOOK II

16.

On Wednesday, November 3, at 3:21 a.m., Susan woke to find a bedbug latched onto her upper arm.

It was perched on the rise of her shoulder, just inches from her face, a brown-black oval, looking for all the world like an apple seed. But it was not an apple seed, or a fleck of paint, or anything else: it was a bedbug, and it was biting her, actively drinking her blood. She felt no pinch, no pain, but the bug was latched on, bent to its task: It was *eating* her—this *thing* was feasting on her flesh.

Feasting. The word caused bile to bubble up from Susan's gut, and she tasted it at the back of her throat. *A monster is feasting on my blood,* she thought stupidly. *A monster.*

She reached up to kill the bedbug, to pluck it off and pulp it between her fingers—and then paused, letting her hand hang in the darkness.

"Alex?" she whispered.

She needed him to see, to know.

"Hey." Louder. "*Alex.*"

He slept as soundly as ever. She twisted her head toward the bug, watching as it drank. She remembered baby Emma nursing, the splotchy yellow infant huffing at her breast, all desperate animal instinct, tugging at her, drawing the fluid free, fat little cheeks plumping and overflowing with milk.

Now *it* was feeding. The bug, this monster, was drinking of her, too.

Again Susan reached for the insect to pluck it free. She formed her fingers into pincers, advanced by millimeters in the dark. She hesitated, dreading the visceral sensation she was sure she'd experience when she grabbed it, the awful little tug and release as she pried the grasping mouth free.

"Alex. *Please.*"

She pushed his back and then shoved it, at last causing him to rustle, clear his throat, and roll over slowly. "Yeah?"

"It's . . ." She looked at her arm. The bug was gone. Her skin was clear, clean, and pale in the darkness.

Alex rubbed his eyes and blinked. "What? Susan?"

"Nothing. Sorry, honey. It's nothing. Go to sleep."

Alex did so, slipping back into unconsciousness, and Susan lay on her side of the bed with her heart hammering, her body awash in adrenalin. The red lines of the bedside clock said 3:27. She went downstairs to wait for dawn.

17.

Alex wasn't convinced.

When he came downstairs in the morning, a few minutes after seven, and Susan tugged down the strap of her Old Navy camisole to show him the tiny pink blemish marring her shoulder, he cocked his head, squinted, and said, "Hmm."

And then, after a moment, he asked if she was sure the mark hadn't been there before.

"No, Alex. It wasn't there before."

"Are you sure? It's not, like, a pimple, or . . . "

"A pimple?"

"Well, whatever. I think I've seen it before."

Susan looked at him. "Alex. I saw the bug. I woke up and saw it biting me. I felt it."

He sighed, said, "Bleh," and pulled open the fridge to rummage around for coffee beans, talking over his shoulder. "It's just . . . I mean, the lady said we were clear, right? The exterminator."

"Dana Kaufmann."

"Right, Kaufmann. I knew a guy with the same name in my dorm, freshman year. Did I ever mention that? *Dan* Kaufmann. Isn't that funny?"

"Alex?"

"Right. Well, she said we didn't have bedbugs. She was pretty unequivocal about it, you said."

There was no way Susan had said that. "Unequivocal" was a word from Alex's lexicon, one of his all-business, look-how-clever-I-am vocabulary words. She rubbed her rutted, scabby wrist with the flat of her palm. "She was wrong, Alex. I'm getting bitten. I think we have to move."

"Whoa, whoa." He pushed shut the fridge door and turned to look at her. "Move? Slow down."

Susan shut her eyes. She saw Jenna staring across the table at Les Halles, insistent: *"I have heard so many horror stories . . . "*

"Alex, I know this sucks."

"No pun intended." Susan didn't laugh, and Alex sighed. "Couldn't it still be something else? What was it the lady—"

"*Kaufmann.*" It was irritating to Susan that Alex couldn't get the name straight. He wasn't paying attention to the problem.

"Right, right. Didn't she say it was spider beetles or something?"

"She said it *could* have been. But it's not. It's bedbugs." She slapped her hand down on the table, loud, and he took a step back, startled, and ended up leaning against the sink. "Alex, I *saw* it."

"I know you did, baby." Alex raised his hands in gentle surrender. He wore baggy pajama bottoms and a ratty, ancient softball jersey. "But you don't think it's possible—just possible, is all I'm saying—that you imagined it? Dreamed it or something? They've really been on your mind lately, right?"

"Well, yeah. Of course they have."

He nodded. Case closed.

"I didn't dream it. It was—it was vivid. It was real."

Alex settled down at the kitchen table across from her. "I know, but moving? Think about it, Susan. I feel like we haven't even unpacked. And it took me a little while, but, you know, I feel like I'm settling in here, I've got the commute down. I like it. And I know you're working hard to figure out a preschool in the area, here, for Emma for the spring."

Crap. In fact, Susan had forgotten about it completely.

"Not to mention that if we have to sacrifice that monster security deposit, we're . . . well, actually, no. I mean, we can't. We can't afford to do that."

"But if we have bedbugs, she'll have to give us the money back."

"Yeah, sure," said Alex. "*If* we can prove it. And anyway, even putting aside the issue of the security deposit, it would cost a few thousand bucks to move again, and we definitely don't have a few thousand extra bucks. Just making rent right now is—I mean, it's fine, we'll be fine, but, you know. Moving is an expensive proposition, especially when you start doing it every couple months."

He went on—calm, reasonable, reassuring—while Susan stared at the ceiling. When he had said his piece, she leaned forward and held his hands in her own.

"I totally know all of that, and I totally see what you're saying." She tried to keep her own voice even and calm, to match his reasonable, rational tone. "Don't forget, this is not the first time. I've been bit before. That's why we called Kaufmann in the first place." She tugged up the sleeves of her pajamas, held up her wrists. "Remember?"

He winced, jerked backward in his chair. "Christ, Sue."

Susan looked down at her wrists. They were red and raw, with angry tracks running in ragged parallel lines from the base of her hand to her elbow. The original cluster of bites was long gone, lost in a muddle of torn, mottled flesh. The whole lower part of her arm looked like a battlefield.

"What the hell have you been doing?"

"Scratching." Susan looked at the floor.

"Scratching?" Gingerly, Alex drew her sleeve back down over her wrist. "Baby, you gotta stop."

"Well, it *itches*."

"Look, Susan—"

"Look, Alex—"

They had both started at the same time, and both stopped at the same time, and he smiled, and Susan found herself smiling, too. She allowed him to take her hands in his. "I know this is upsetting," he began. "But can we give it a few days and just see what happens? As soon as you have a bite, or I have a bite, or God forbid Emma does, we'll tell Andrea."

God forbid Emma does. God forbid—

"Forget telling Andrea. If Emma has a bite, we're leaving right away."

"Well, Andrea may want to solve the problem for us."

"Are you kidding, Alex? She hasn't even fixed the floor, or the outlet cover, or . . . Andrea's useless. You were right about her in the first place. She's a useless landlord."

"OK, so then we'll move. We will. If we have to, we'll figure it out. I promise."

The Mr. Coffee beeped, and Alex stood abruptly to pour himself a cup. Susan was imagining Andrea, poor old Andrea, nodding, stoic but brokenhearted when presented with the news that they were leaving. She remembered the feel of the shaky old hand resting on her elbow, the two of them enjoying a mother-daughter kind of moment on the stoop that afternoon, partners in some unnameable melancholy.

"So that's the plan," Alex said, pouring his coffee and smiling gently. "We give it a few days. If we so much as hear a bug farting in the night, we are out of here."

Susan sighed. She knew what he was doing; kicking the can down the road, giving her time to forget this flight of fancy when a few days had gone by. It had happened before. When she had wanted to get a dog; when she had made noises about leaving New York, moving upstate, somewhere with mountains. He would say, hmm, let's think about it, hmm, we'll talk about it next week, when I'm not so crazy at work, when Emma's not sick, whatever . . . and eventually other things cropped up to distract her attention. She looked at her shoulder. The pink mark on her arm was tiny, barely visible. Maybe it *was* a pimple. And they *had* brought in a professional, paid good money for a thorough investigation not two weeks ago, and been given the all clear.

But the fresh knot of unease that had formed in her chest that morning at three o'clock, when she woke to see the monster on her shoulder—*it was no dream, no dream at all*—had not abated. It throbbed, sending out one message, over and over: they had to move, had to get out of there, and quick.

Or else or else or else.

Alex turned to look at the clock, and Susan gnawed furtively at her nails, wrenching off a hunk of thumbnail and spitting it on the floor. A pulse of pain shot up her thumb, and blood welled where the nail had been and drooled down over the knuckle. Alex turned back and planted a sweet kiss on her cheek. "So, we'll handle it. We're on top of it."

"OK," she said and smiled weakly, rubbing her eyes. "OK."

Clutching his coffee cup, Alex padded upstairs to get ready for his day. As soon as he disappeared, Susan's shoulder began to itch.

18.

When Marni arrived for work, an hour and a half later, Alex had just left, and Susan heard him on the exterior stairs, greeting the nanny in passing. She had remained in the kitchen, slowly sipping her coffee and staring with dead eyes out the front windows.

"Hey," Marni called brightly from the front door, and Susan leaned back in the chair to respond.

"Morning. Emma's upstairs."

Marni poked her head into the kitchen, and the girl's big brown eyes and tousled auburn hair were framed by the morning sunlight like a shampoo commercial. "You all right, Susan?"

"Yeah. I'm fine."

Susan smiled tightly. Marni was so effortlessly beautiful, and she could only imagine what she herself must look like: unshowered and exhausted, her hair a knotted mess, her eyes red rimmed, her face unmade-up and greasy.

"Marni!" Emma squealed from upstairs. "I'm making a pee-pee, Marni!"

"Awesome!" Marni yelled. "Here I come!" She bounded out of the kitchen toward the stairs, flashing an *ain't-she-cute?* grin over her shoulder as she went.

Susan rose and trudged up behind her, wondering about the moment a few minutes earlier, when Marni had brushed past Alex outside the apartment on the stairway landing. It was a small space. How close had they passed? Had her small perky breasts pressed against his chest? Had Alex gotten a deep noseful of her flirty orange-blossom perfume? How often did they squeeze past each other that way, while Susan was upstairs picking out Emma's clothes or downstairs pouring milk on cereal? Marni was immortal, impervious to tiredness or hurt. She was like Alex in that way, Susan reflected sourly: both of them wore the mantle of the world so lightly. Not the type to get sunburned, or stung by bees, or suffer the untimely death of their mothers.

Susan climbed the steps until she stood on the landing between the bedrooms, watching Marni get Emma dressed. Her eyes lingered on her daughter's naked body: her clear vanilla skin, the bulge of her tummy, the fragile lines of her legs, the small pink creases of her nipples.

"Hey, Em? Do you feel itchy?"

Emma looked up and giggled, like it was a joke. "No, I do not."

Marni laughed and Emma waggled her head playfully, but Susan didn't say, "Good puppy," like she was supposed to. She nodded silently, slowly, and went back down the stairs to the kitchen.

*

Susan turned on her MacBook and drummed her fingers on the kitchen table until the screen lit up, telling herself all the while that she was being an idiot. *Go take a shower*, she told herself. *Put on something pretty, get the hell outside.* It was really a great area—the Promenade, the cute coffee shops on Smith Street, that row of antique-furniture stores

along Atlantic Avenue. Outside the kitchen windows of 56 Cranberry Street the day had blossomed bright and blue, the kind of crystal blue you only get on crisp autumn days, when smoky clouds drift
through pockets of sunlight.

Go paint something, for God's sake. Capture the autumn light. Eat a bagel.

Instead, Susan stayed rooted to her kitchen chair, drinking coffee and surfing the Internet, her face bathed in the pale light of the
screen. She Googled "bedbugs" and "bedbug infestation" and "signs
of bedbug infestation," scanned the resulting paragraphs, and jumped
from link to link. She downloaded an article from the *Journal of Ap-
plied Entomology*, scrolled through chat-room threads, and watched
YouTube clips of bedbugs swarming in laboratory jars.

"Yick," said Susan.

When the coffeepot was empty she brewed more.

Susan learned that bedbugs can be killed by extremes of heat
and cold; she learned that they hide in the hair of their victims, in dis-
carded clothes, under beds, and in couch cushions. Back on Bed-
bugDemolition.com, Susan discovered numerous schools of thought
relating to bedbug control. Some exterminators adhered to the aggressive methods of Dana Kaufmann: contact kill, residual kill, growth
control. Some advocated the exclusive use of pyrethroids; others suggested more traditional insecticides or a compound made of diatomaceous earth, which could be purchased at pet-supply stores and
which, when sprinkled around the home, kills the bugs by drying
out their waxy membranes.

"DDT!!!!!!" suggested one contributor, who signed himself
EndsJustifyMeans. It was noted in a flurry of responses that DDT
was banned in the United States in 1972, one contributor sneeringly
adding, "SILENT SPRING MUCH, DUMBASS?" To which the

stubborn EndsJustifyMeans simply wrote "**<u>DDT!!!!!!</u>**" again, this time all in bold and underlined.

The guy who signed himself 0-684-84328-5@gmail.com had contributed to this thread, too, writing "makesureit'sreallybedbugs." Susan wrinkled her brow and grunted, "Huh," when she had teased out this jammed-together phrasing. What does he mean, "make sure it's really bedbugs"? She clicked on the signature link and dashed off a quick e-mail to 0-684-84328-5@gmail.com: "So how you do you know it's really bedbugs?"

As she plowed through website after website, Susan occasionally scratched at her wrists and shoulder. At some point, the shoulder-bite itch intensified, and she dug a ballpoint pen out of the junk drawer and used its capped end to zero in on the itch. At 11:52, her phone rang, startling her with its crazy rattling vibration on the counter. The screen showed that it was Karen Grossbard, a college friend, who was in town for the weekend with her two kids; they had made loose plans, a couple weeks earlier, to hang out today. Susan was absorbed in a detailed explanation of the dual proboscis morphology of bedbugs and other hemipterans: one channel to suck the victim's blood, the other to inject saliva and anticoagulant, which maximized the flow of blood while keeping the host from feeling the sting.

Keeping her eyes locked on the article, Susan fumbled for the phone and silenced the call.

*

Another sign of a bedbug infestation, according to a contributor to BedbugDemolition.com named MrMcEschars, was their deposited feces. "Gross but true!" MrMcEschars wrote and attached a picture of one such deposit in his bathroom: a small pile of black and brown dust. Five minutes later, Susan was yawning elaborately, stretching back in her chair and twisting her torso, when she spotted a pile of the feces on the kitchen counter, just below the broken outlet cover. She blinked, gasped, and froze, staring at it in shock.

Finally, she rose slowly, walked over to the counter, and poked gingerly at the pile with the tip of her ring finger.

Coffee grounds.

"Oh, for God's sake," Susan said to no one. She exhaled heavily as her heart resumed beating. She was brushing the coffee grounds off the counter and into her palm when she heard keys jingling in the door, followed by Emma's hopeful call of "Mama?"

She called, "In here, love!" as she rinsed the coffee grounds off her hand into the sink.

Her legs were wobbly beneath her, dancing with pinpricks. She had been in the kitchen, seated at her computer, since the girls left, five and a half hours earlier.

*

"Hey, you want to know what I read on the Internet?" Susan said.

"That the Internet is a giant waste of time?"

"Har-dee-har."

The TV was on in the background, with Alex keeping one eye on the *Top Chef* season finale. When they spoke on the phone at 5:30, Alex had announced his intention to make a big chef's salad for dinner, but Susan told him the lettuce had a lot of rotten pieces, so could he grab a pizza on his way home, instead? She was lying about the lettuce. In fact, she had seen small dark specks on the bottom of the vegetable drawer, and, even after confirming that they were apple seeds, and after rinsing the drawer thoroughly, she couldn't shake the idea that the spots had been dead bedbugs.

"All right, sorry. What did you read on the Internet?"

"I learned that a lot of people with bedbugs think they've killed them—they think the infestation is over, in other words, and then the bugs come back." Alex chewed his pizza, half listening, while Susan yawned into her fist. That afternoon she'd taken Emma to the big playground down in Dumbo and watched her make circuits from the rope ladder to the slide and back, too exhausted and preoccupied to give chase.

"They're not like ants, where you just use Raid or whatever and they're gone. Even in abandoned apartments, with no one to eat from, bedbugs can live for months and months. Some people say up to a *year*. Oh, and they can hide in your hair. Disgusting, right?"

"Yes," said Alex, and made a face. "Actually . . . wait . . . " He put down his slice, dug his fingers into his corkscrew curls, his features convulsed with exaggerated terror. "I . . . I . . . feel them right now! Aaaaah!"

He shook his head wildly, clutching at his temples.

Susan looked at him evenly. "I need you to take this seriously, OK?"

"I am. Seriously, honey. I totally am. In fact, I called Dana Kaufmann today."

Susan's heart leapt in her chest. "You did?"

"I did. Could you pass me another slice of the mushroom?"

She obeyed, her hands trembling slightly. *Yes! Let Kaufmann come back. This time she would see—surely, this time . . .*

"I just figured we might as well have her come back and take another look," Alex said. "She wasn't too happy about it. She told me

she was 'past the point of reasonable doubt as to that particular resi-
dence.' Quote, unquote."

Susan smiled. It was easy to imagine the deadpan Dana Kaufmann using exactly those words, and in exactly the icy tone Alex had
conjured. Alex smiled back, took a big bite of his fresh slice, and
tugged a strand of cheese from the corner of his mouth. "Anyway, I
talked her into it. I told her my wife is pretty sure we've got bedbugs
now, even if we didn't before, and my wife's a pretty smart lady."

"Thank you." Susan reached over and stroked Alex's cheek gently. "I really appreciate it."

"I'm on your side, babe." There was a pause, and then he delivered the punchline. "Hey, can I borrow two hundred bucks? Tax free
if we pay in cash."

Susan laughed and helped herself to a piece of pizza while Alex
started in about his day. Slowly but surely, he said, things were turning around for GemFlex. "Bottom line, we might remain midlist for
a little while, but to tell you the truth, that's *fine*. Midlist is *fine*."

"Of course it is," Susan said.

"I mean, so we're snapping a few Rolexes instead of Cartier, who
cares?"

"Exactly."

"Although, actually, on Friday afternoon we booked a gig with
Tiffany—"

"Oo-la-la."

"I know. So, who the hell knows?"

When Alex asked Susan what she'd done with her morning, she
took a breath and said, "Oh, you know. I took a walk, did some
sketching on the Promenade. I'm going to get back in there and do
some painting soon."

"That's great, honey."

They cleared the table, and Susan sat sipping wine while Alex put in a tray of fish sticks so Marni would have something to give Emma for lunch the next day. When a decent amount of time had passed, Susan changed the subject back to the bedbugs.

"So, I'm sorry. When did Kaufmann say she was coming back?"

"Uh, I wrote it down. Friday at 4:30, I think."

Susan nodded, tried to smile. It was now Wednesday night, and Friday at 4:30 seemed like an awfully long way away.

"And look," Alex went on. "If she finds anything, then we'll decide what to do."

If she finds anything . . . Susan felt a cold rush of fear in her spine. *What if she doesn't?*

*

Four hours later, Susan was standing at the linen closet, gathering up a couple of sheets, a pillowcase, and their spare blanket, when Alex stuck his head out of the bedroom.

"Hey. What are you doing? You're sleeping on the sofa?"

"Yeah. I know, I know." She laughed, trying to sound light and self-teasing. She had thought Alex was already asleep. "I think, for now, I'll just be more comfortable."

Alex made a pouty face and looked like he was about to argue. But then he shrugged. "OK, babe."

She walked down the steps to the front hall, clutching her ungainly camp-out bundle tightly to her chest, and then looked back up at Alex at the top of the steps. They stood that way for a long moment, her looking up and him looking down, and from Susan's perspective he was silhouetted by the wash of light from the bath-room behind him. Her husband looked a distant stranger, dimly per-ceived from a mile away.

*

Susan inspected the sofa thoroughly before lying down, of course. A contributor on BedbugDemolition.com named EcdysisMan had written a chilling vignette about (finally) clearing his gorgeous double bed of bedbugs, only to have an overnight guest discover a thriving colony between the cushions of the sofa. Susan lifted the cushions one by one, shook them out, banged them together, slipped her fingers into the cases and wriggled them around. Nothing.

She dry swallowed an Ambien, lay down, and descended imme-diately into a vortex of anxiety.

Alex would see, wouldn't he? He'd have to see. It was ridiculous to stay in an apartment that had bedbugs—*if there were bugs, if it's real, what if it's*—over a matter of a couple thousand bucks. It was insane. She could call her dad, ask him to borrow the money, to help them out with the move.

No way . . . come on, Susan . . .

Her dad didn't have money and wouldn't be inclined to loan it if he did. Alex's parents were the ones with the money, and they had given Alex a ton to go to art school—money that he was supposedly paying back, although Susan couldn't remember the last time they had made a payment. The room felt hot, too hot, but when she kicked her leg out from under the blanket she felt a draft, so she tucked it away again. Beads of sweat formed on her temples and dripped down into her eyes, convincing her for one alarming instant that bugs were crawling across her eyelids. She wiped away the sweat and stared at the ceiling.

At least it's a different ceiling for a change.

Small sounds drifted up the air shaft from Andrea's apartment: shuffling, slippered footsteps, the clink of a spoon on a teacup. She was reminded of the weird *ping* they had heard—whatever had happened with that? *I guess Andrea took care of it. . . .*

Of all the flaws with the apartment, all the things Susan had complained of, it was the only one Andrea had done something about.

When at last she slept, Susan had horrible torturing nightmares of bedbugs. They were marching across her stomach, leaving behind them a trail of that disgusting brown-black dust—*feces.* A trail of bug shit on her body like the uneven black line of an Etch-a-Sketch. They scuttled up her stomach and bit her chest, her shoulders, her neck and face. In the dream she couldn't lift her arms to wipe them away, could only lie helpless as they sank their horrid needle-noses into her undefended flesh—stinging—pinching—*biting*—and then, *disappearing*, skittering back to the air shaft, crawling into the cracks between the glass and the wall—

She opened her eyes, gasped for breath, rose unsteadily from the sofa and staggered across the room. She slapped at her body, ran her fingers across her chest—no bugs. No marks. Nothing. It had be a dream, this time—*right?*

It had to be.

In the darkness, she pressed her face against one of the little windows on the air shaft, trying to see down.

19.

When she woke it was still dark, and Susan was on the floor, wrapped in a starchy linen tablecloth they'd gotten as a wedding present from Alex's great-aunt and never used. Susan had no memory of taking the tablecloth out of the sideboard, nor of deciding to sleep on the ground. Her back was sore and knotted, her eyes ached in their sockets, and her mouth tasted like ash. Rubbing at her temples with her thumb and forefinger, Susan stumbled from the living room down the hall to the kitchen, where she glanced at the clock on the stove. It was 6:22 in the morning.

She trudged up the stairs, scratching absently at her wrist. Halfway up the stairs, she heard Alex's alarm go off and felt a pang of longing—now he would snooze for ten minutes, and it would be so pleasant to slip into the bed, to nuzzle her face into his neck and snooze alongside him. Instead, she went into the bathroom, peed, and flushed.

She stood, shuffled over to the sink and was squeezing toothpaste out of the tube when she saw a tiny translucent blob nestled among the bristles. Susan blinked. Her mouth dropped open. Slowly, she raised the toothbrush and brought it closer to her face, squinting.

It was an egg. She recognized it from a dozen different images she had stared at on BedbugDemolition.com. A milky white larval orb, smaller than a pinhead, nestled between two bristles of her toothbrush.

But she could *see* it. In the bright vanity lights of the bathroom mirror there was no ambiguity; it wasn't the middle of the night, it wasn't dark, and she wasn't half asleep. Susan was wide awake, and she was staring at a birth sac, in which, she knew, a baby bedbug waited to emerge.

"Mother*fucker*," she whispered.

Susan reached carefully with her forefinger and thumb, feeling for the impossibly small white dot. She grasped it, raised her fingers slowly, opened her hand—and saw nothing.

"Shit. Shit shit shit."

She must have accidentally brushed the egg away, into the sink. "Shit!" Quickly, Susan pulled the stopper of the sink closed, so the tiny sac couldn't slip down the drain. She craned her neck over the basin, squinting for the white dot against the off-white ceramic. Nothing.

"Damn it!" Susan said. *"Damn it."*

"Baby? You all right?"

"What?"

Alex had cracked open the bathroom door and leaned in to the room, groggy and unshaven. Susan looked over, holding the toothbrush limply in her hand.

"I just asked if you were all right?"

"Yeah. I . . . " She turned back to the sink, playing out the conversation in her mind:

"There was an egg sac on my toothbrush."

"Oh, wow. Let me see it."

"It's gone. I lost it."

"Well, if you see another one, let me know."

"It's nothing," Susan said, and Alex shrugged.

"Okey-doke."

"You need to pee?"

On the way out of the bathroom, Susan flung her toothbrush into the trash.

*

By the time Alex emerged from the bathroom, Susan had dressed and returned downstairs; when he came down to make his coffee, she asked if he could hang out with Emma that morning till Marni arrived. A cloud of annoyance passed over Alex's face, and Susan could see him weighing the value of his lost work hours against the cost of pissing her off. Finally, he smiled, shot her a thumbs-up, and said, "Of course, baby."

"Great."

Susan pulled on her coat, suddenly desperate to get out of the house and taste the air.

"You doing all right?" Alex paused on the stairs, examining her as he took his first slow sip of coffee. "How was sleeping on the sofa?"

"Fine."

"Oh, good. So I'll survive if and when you kick me out of bed."

Susan gave him a tight smile in lieu of a laugh and slipped out of the apartment, buttoning her coat as she walked down the exterior stairs to Cranberry Street. Immediately, she realized that the weather was too cold for her shortish skirt, loose cotton top, and light jacket; the wind bit at her legs, chased up her skirt and her sleeves.

This was autumn weather, and Susan felt a melancholy shiver, like the seasons had changed without asking her permission. She glanced back at 56 Cranberry Street but kept on walking.

She stopped into a characterless deli on Henry Street, ordered an everything bagel with scallion cream cheese, and ate it as she walked the streets. For an hour, then two hours, she walked around Brooklyn in wide circles, watching the sun come up and the commuters emerge from their apartments and move in their intersecting tides toward the various subways. She meandered as far south as 2nd Place, west to the Atlantic Center, east as far as the shipyards. At 9:30 she was on Van Brunt Street, on the outskirts of Red Hook, and she stopped into a consignment shop that was just opening for the day; there was a poster taped in the window of a cartoon bedbug, upside down with its legs in the air. "Every item treated for infestation!" it said. Susan had a sudden, insane fear that this guarantee was backed up by infrared cameras, scanning each patron for bugs, and that some sort of alarm bell would sound as bedbug-sniffing dogs chased her from the store.

"Don't be an idiot," she muttered and forced herself to remain in the store for fifteen minutes, rifling through the racks of vintage dresses and antique costume jewelry.

Then Susan just kept walking, trudging in no particular direction, yawning, shivering, her bone-deep exhaustion making her feel like she was walking on the bottom of the ocean. Pressure throbbed behind her eyes. She weaved down Smith Street in a haze, trying to puzzle out what was happening to the house . . . to *her*. The dreams, the bites, the egg on her toothbrush that morning that had disappeared before she could snatch it, before Alex could see it . . . she felt like the bugs were teasing *her*—tormenting *her*—like they had somehow singled her out for punishment . . .

. . . and don't forget about Jessie—good old Jessie Spender . . .

"Hey! Watch it, lady!"

Susan had collided with a knot of people clustered at the corner of Schermerhorn and Court, in front of the state courthouse. They were gawking at a woman in a bright orange jumpsuit and hand-cuffs, being led from a prison van into the courthouse by a trio of brutish-looking female police officers. Susan brought a trembling hand up to her chest. The prisoner was Anna Mara Phelps, who had shoved her poor babies to their death from the rooftop on Livingston Street.

At the door of the courthouse, the prisoner stopped in her shuf-fling progress and turned to stare back at the crowd, her eyes wide and innocent and terrified.

Susan found herself staring directly at Anna Mara. "It's OK," she mouthed to the terrified woman, who looked so small and fragile surrounded by the escorting officers and the restless crowd, like a trapped bird. *"It's OK."* Anna Mara looked back at her desperately before being led away. Susan turned and stumbled down the street.

Strange words appeared again in Susan's head, flashed before her eyes like neon on a dark street: *not only on blood—on body and soul.*

Susan didn't know what it was, but something very wrong was going on, and she had to act.

*

"Oh, my God, Susan! I was just *talking* about you!"

"Really?"

Susan reached the intersection of Schermerhorn and Court Street and waited at the light, running her tongue over her dry and chapped lips, while Jenna prattled in her ear. "I was just saying to Rami—do you remember Rami? He's the choreographer on *Dig-nity*, and his boyfriend went to college with you, actually—anyway, I was just telling Rami all about you, and how I *seriously* owed you a call."

"That's sweet. How're you doing, Jenna?" Susan cleared her throat, trying to let some light and air into her voice. "Did that show open?"

"What? Yeah. We got—there was a pretty good review in the *Times*, actually." In the background, someone, she guessed Rami, screeched "*Pretty* good?" with exaggerated incredulity.

"Oh, I'm sorry. I totally missed it."

"That's OK. You're so busy."

"Jenna . . . " Susan took a deep breath and steadied herself in the doorway of the Barnes & Noble. She winced at the reflection, haunted and haggard, staring back at her from the bookstore's glass doorway. "I need to ask you a favor."

It was no use. She could hear and feel the tears in her voice; surely Jenna could hear them as well.

"Susan? What's up?"

The wind had intensified along the broad stretch of Court Street. It whistled and whipped at her ears. Susan held the phone closer and drew her coat closed around her chest. "Me and Emma need a place to crash."

She ended with a hopeful rise in her voice and waited for eager, generous Jenna to say, "Oh, of course!" Or "No problem!" Or "I'll leave the keys with the doorman. . . . "

Instead there was only silence, and the light crackle of an imperfect connection.

"Jenna?" she said at last.

"What's going on?" Jenna's voice on the other end dropped to a whisper. "Is it the bedbugs?"

"Oh, no, no." Susan spoke quickly, rattling out the words, her voice rising desperately. "Actually, no, remember? Kaufmann said we don't have them, I thought I told you, I could have sworn I told you,

and by the way thanks so much for the recommendation. She was—
that was super helpful."

Another silence. The tinny echo of the cell-phone connection.
The wind whipped up into Susan's sleeves. "No, it's not that. It's, um,
it's Alex. We're having a really hard time."

"Oh. No kidding?"

Susan bobbed her head up and down as she lied. Except, it was
true, wasn't it? They *were* having a hard time.

"Yeah, so, we're working it out, you know, but it's pretty bad
right now. So, I mean, can I—can we—can Emma and I please come
crash with you for a few days? Just till I figure out our next step."

Finally Susan shut up, tilted her head back up to the sky, and
squeezed her eyes shut. *Come on, Jenna. Come on.*

"I . . . oh, Sue." The final silence was the longest. Susan felt a tear
spill down her cheek, before Jenna spoke at last. "I can't get bedbugs.
I just can't."

Susan ended the call and shoved her phone in her pocket, curs-
ing loudly and stomping her foot.

"Ma'am?"

At some point she had entered the Barnes & Noble and was
standing at the table of new releases. A small crowd of perplexed
shoppers were looking her up and down, and a rent-a-cop security
guard placed a gentle but firm hand on her shoulder.

"Sorry," Susan muttered, and pushed her way out of the store.

*

On the way home she stopped at a pet store and asked if they
sold diatomaceous earth, the crumbly soil compound that was one of

several supposed bedbug killers she had read about on BedbugDe-molition.com. The saleswoman, a puffy, overly made-up woman in her fifties, chuckled ruefully. "Sure, honey. You're lucky we still have some in stock."

"Oh, yeah?"

"You think you're the only one with bedbugs?"

Susan felt a hot rush of shame and looked furtively around the shop. "No, I . . . I . . ." She had no idea what other uses one might have for diatomaceous earth. The pet-shop lady shook her head and grinned.

"Don't worry, dear. Everybody's got the darn things, or it sure seems like it."

"Not like I do," Susan muttered. The saleswoman cocked her head and said, "Sorry, dear?" But Susan just shook her head and forked over the $27.50 for her three-pound bag.

"Well, I wish you luck, sweetheart, I do," said the saleswoman. After giving Susan her change, she squirted hand sanitizer into her palm from a dispenser beside the cash register. "Do you know where you got 'em?"

"No, I . . . " Susan trailed off, and her mouth dropped open.

"Ma'am?"

It was funny—for all her research, all her terror, it had never oc-curred to Susan to wonder where the bedbugs had come from. But as soon as the woman asked, Susan knew the answer. She took her bag and left the store, passing under the tinkling shop bell, clutching the heavy bag of soil to her chest. Susan marched up Court Street and turned left onto Montague toward home.

20.

Quietly, Susan let herself into the apartment and set down her lumpy package of diatomaceous earth just inside the door. She poked her head into the kitchen, then slipped off her shoes and padded in her socks to the living room, where she found Marni dozing on the sofa, her phone dangling in one hand, breathing lightly.

"I can't believe it," Susan whispered to herself. "I can't believe it took so long to figure this out."

Marni's chest rose and fell gently; her thick copper hair lay in a tumble across the pillow.

Every day she's been coming here. Every day, in my home. With my daughter.

Staring at the sleeping girl, Susan dragged the nails of her right hand along her left wrist, harder and harder, perforating the barely healed skin for the hundredth time, drawing out bright red beads of blood.

Every single day.

"Marni," she said sharply. "Get up."

Susan waited a moment and then knelt at the girl's side and shook her, roughly, by the shoulders. Marni proved to be a lighter sleeper than Alex—she jerked awake, blinked twice, smiling through her confusion. "Oh, hey, Sue. Emma's napping." She fumbled for the baby monitor, which sat on the coffee table, and lifted it up reassur-ingly. "Poor thing was totally zonked. We went over to the carousel, and then . . . um, Susan?"

Susan was still crouching beside the sofa, staring at Marni, not moving. She could almost see them, the bedbugs, stage-one and stage-two nymphs most likely, invisible to the naked eye, crawling out from Marni's shirtsleeves, up from her cleavage, marching in un-even lines. Bugs appearing from the folds and creases of the girl's clothing, tumbling onto the sofa, disappearing into the cracks, slid-ing between the floorboards. It was disgusting.

"Marni, you have to leave."

"Oh." She hefted herself up to a sitting position. "Wait. What?"

"I'm sorry," said Susan. "But it's not working out."

"What? What do you mean?"

"You're fired. Get out. Right now."

Marni's eyes were wide with pretended innocence. Susan felt waves of hatred and disgust wash over her. The girl shifted on the sofa, ran a hand through her hair, and Susan saw the invisible rain of them, bedbugs floating like dandruff off her scalp. She grasped Marni by the wrists. "Get up. Please. Please, just go."

"But why? What is this about?

Susan's mounting distaste crested, transforming into pure hot fury. "Why?" Susan laughed once, a high thin bark. "What is this *about*?" Like she didn't *know*! Like she didn't go home every night and laugh at them—laugh at *her*, laugh at *Susan*, laugh at what she'd done to her. "Because you're *dirty*."

Marni's back stiffened, and she stared at Susan with cold, hard eyes. "Excuse me?"

"Because you're *disgusting*!" Susan heard the hateful words pouring out of her mouth, a hot torrent of bitter words, but she couldn't stop them. Didn't want to stop. "Because you got bedbugs in some 10th Avenue motel room, or at your Friday night gang bang—"

"Oh, my God! Susan!"

"—and you brought them here. Into my house! You contaminated my home!"

Susan was shrieking now. She felt her blood pumping in her veins; her hands were clutched into fists, her ragged fingernails biting like teeth into the tender flesh of her palms. The pain felt good and powerful, clean and right. Marni was furiously collecting her things, sweeping her computer and hair-ties and a textbook into her backpack.

"This is unbelievable," she said. "*Unbelievable.*"

"Out! I want you out!" Susan chased Marni as she stomped down the hallway. "Get *out!*"

She reached past Marni, threw open the door, and it cracked against the wall of the landing.

"Fine!" shouted Marni. "Jesus! Fine!"

Susan slammed the door behind her and locked it. Through the wall she heard the muffled tromp of Marni's footsteps as they rapidly descended the interior stairs. As Susan stood there heaving hard raspy breaths, she felt something at the back of her knees: A bite. She whirled around, slapped at her legs, trying to catch the dirty little creature in the act. Another one, this time right at the corner of her eye. She brought her hand up, pinched at where she had felt the insect, clawed at her face.

When she looked up, Emma was standing halfway down the steps, clutching Mr. Boogle, scratching her little bottom and looking around the room.

"Mama? Did Marni go home?"

"Oh, baby."

"Is everything OK, Mama?"

"Yes, honey. We're fine. Everything is fine."

She smiled at Emma, who smiled sleepily back, Mr. Boogle dangling against her pink thigh. "All right, Mama."

"Everything is fine and dandy like sugar candy."

*

Susan spent the next two hours spreading her diatomaceous earth around the apartment. She crawled into the closets and sprinkled loose handfuls of the stuff along the baseboards; she worked her way down the steps, layering a line of chalky soil along the joints and cracks as she went. Emma passed these hours in front of the television, enjoying the unimaginable treat of a *Sesame Street* marathon, lazing like a pasha in a nest of pillows—Susan having decided that the sofa was off-limits for the time being.

At a little past 4:30 Susan was squatting in front of the kitchen sink. The bag, now half empty, dangled from one hand while she seized handfuls of earth with the other, patting them behind and around the small bucket she'd set up for compostable material. At the sudden, heavy sound of a knock at the door, she twisted around, like a dog startled by the sudden noise, and rose unsteadily to answer it.

"Heya," asked Louis. "Whatcha got there?" He angled his head to the bag Susan clutched to her chest.

"Nothing," said Susan, and she took an unsteady step backward into the apartment. "What's up?"

Susan needed to get back to her task. There were many corners of the house she had not yet reached with her bag of diatomaceous earth. She wanted it scattered everywhere the bugs could be. She wanted to decimate their population, poison their habitats, run them down.

"Well, this is going to sound . . ." Louis grinned shyly, like he was going to ask her to the prom. He looked down, tracing a nervous pattern on the rug of the landing with the toe of his boot. "The thing is, Susan, I'm a little worried about you."

"Worried?"

"Well, listen, this afternoon, I was sweeping some leaves from the front stoop, and I saw that girl go sprinting out of here . . ."

Susan let him trail off.

"Anyway, so. I hemmed and hawed about it, but I figured I'd just come and make sure everything was copacetic in apartment number two."

"I fired the babysitter, that's all. Everything is fine." Susan readjusted her fingers on the mouth of the bag, and the foil package crinkled in her grip.

"Glad to hear it," said Louis, nodding slowly, trying to look past her, into the apartment. From the TV in the living room they could hear Elmo's falsetto giggle. "And your little girl, she's doing all right?"

"Yes, Louis." Susan felt like her whole body was vibrating, could feel the bag of loose soil trembling in her hand. *What the hell did he want?*

"Listen." Louis said suddenly, quietly, leaning forward toward her. "Is it bedbugs?"

"Bedbugs?" Susan dropped the bag, and her eyes shot open. "Why would you say that?"

"Whoa, whoa." Louis reached forward to pat her reassuringly, and she flinched backward from the touch. "No reason, really. It's just that you asked me about them. You were awfully worried, seems like. And I just know, bedbugs, boy . . . that's the sort of thing people get themselves all worked up over. All twisted up in knots. Hate to see that happen to you."

He was just being nosy. He didn't know anything. Couldn't help her. Nobody could help her.

"Really," said Susan, beginning to inch the door shut. "I'm fine."

*

Susan glanced in to check on Emma—rapt, thumb-in-mouth, Mr. Boogle tucked under one arm—and returned to the kitchen. Louis's and Andrea's voices echoed from the front stoop, a low murmur of old-person argument drifting up through the slightly cracked kitchen window.

"... it's a free country," Louis was saying, "and if there's something I can do . . . a person having trouble or . . . "

Susan watched through the window. Andrea was shaking her head, waving a nagging finger up at Louis, who had six inches on her. The wind carried away her words, and Susan just caught scraps, drifting up through the window: " . . . your own beeswax . . . bothering *me* is one thing . . . nobody wants some old . . . "

Susan scowled, shut the kitchen window, and moved on to the closet in the front hall.

21.

"Sorry, will you tell me again what it's called?"

"Diatomaceous earth."

Alex was at the kitchen table, eating dinner. He had made chicken parmesan, and Susan had eaten three bites before thanking him and returning to her project—she had forgotten about the pantry, of course there could be bedbugs in the pantry, why not?

"And it's . . . what is it? Like, fancy dirt?"

Susan, pulling out boxes of macaroni and cheese so she could get to the back of the cabinet, recited from memory what it said on BedbugDemolition.com. "Diatomaceous earth sticks to the waxed shells of bedbugs and draws out the moisture, and the bugs die shortly thereafter."

Alex sipped his beer and spoke hesitantly. "So, what's the story here, baby? Have you actually seen any bedbugs since yesterday? Yes? No?"

Reaching into the darkness of the cabinet to crumble out a fistful of the powder, Susan grinned sardonically. *Not that I can show you, Alex. Not that will meet your standard of proof.* "No," she said flatly, withdrawing her hand from the pantry. "I have not."

"Oh." Alex exhaled. "Good, good. That's good. Hey, so Susan . . . do you have plans for tomorrow morning?"

"Plans?" What was this? "No."

"Well, I was thinking I'd take the morning off. We have that Tiffany shoot at 3:30, but Vic can handle the prep. I thought maybe I'd take you over to a doctor. So someone can take a look at those bites of yours—or, or, whatever they are."

"A doctor?" Susan shifted on her haunches and pulled open another cabinet. "I guess. What about Emma?"

"Well, won't she be with Marni?"

"Marni doesn't work for us anymore."

*

Susan knew from BedbugDemolition.com that bedbugs are attracted not only to carbon dioxide but to body heat and will strike, night after night, at any stretch of exposed skin.

And so, after Alex went to sleep that night, Susan found a pair of his long underwear and pulled it up over her own. She dug out a long flannel nightgown from the bottom of a drawer and pulled it over her head, tugging the sleeves down as far as they could go, and then rolled on a pair of woolen socks up over the cuffs of the long underwear. Finally she tucked her hair under a shower cap and, after a moment's hesitation, slipped on a pair of thick winter gloves.

"Well," she asked the mirror in the bathroom off the kitchen. "How do I look?"

Pretty much like a lunatic, she answered herself silently. But there was nothing to be done about it. Susan took two and a half Ambien with a cup of water, lay down on her back on the floor of the living room, and closed her eyes.

*

Approximately three and a half hours later, at 3:40 a.m. on Friday, November 5, Susan awoke to the sensation of being choked.

She sat up, coughing, grabbing at her throat.

There was something crawling in her mouth, way at the back, on the slippery edge where the tongue takes root. She coughed, cleared her throat, hacking like a cat. She felt the tiny feet skittering around in the back of her mouth.

Oh my God oh my God Oh my—

She stuck two fingers into her throat and scrabbled madly for the thing, trying to pluck at it, get it out, get it out—her fingers slipped across the wet surface of her tongue. But the bug was too fast, it evaded her searching fingers, danced around in maddening circles. *Or, God, was it just one, was there more than one? How many—*

Susan jammed her fingers farther in, bruising the back of her throat. Stomach acids rose up, burned her esophagus. Tears of pain and shock welled in her eyes.

After thirty terrible seconds, Susan hacked, gagged violently, and swallowed the bedbug. Then she heaved herself to her feet and raced to the kitchen sink to vomit. As the yellow and orange sick pooled in the sink, she drew up the stopper; pinching her nose closed with one hand, she sifted through the vomit with the other, trying to find the tiny bug in the vile puddle.

No luck. Of course.

Susan rinsed out her mouth three times with water and then gingerly reached with a fingertip to touch the welt she already felt rising on the back of her tongue. She almost gagged again and had to stop, but when she swallowed she could feel it, could picture it, rising red and round way at the back of her mouth—out of sight.

She could tell Alex. She could go upstairs, and—*if* she could get him to wake up, *if* she could get him to pay attention—there was zero chance that he would believe her. And why *should* he believe her? He wouldn't be able to see this new mark. It was hidden, just like the bugs wanted it to be.

Susan poured herself a glass of wine, sat down at the kitchen table, and turned on her computer.

*

When Safari opened, some vestigial reflex led Susan to check her Facebook page, and her eyes dimly scrolled through the mundane and mock-profound information displayed by old friends. Leslie Clover was remarrying her ex-husband. Sean Hurley was about to publish a book of poems with a small press in Nebraska. Someone was having a baby; someone had eaten at the Applebee's in Times Square; someone had been hired to teach economics at NYU. These all felt like dispatches from some distant land where Susan had once lived, a long time ago.

She typed in the address for BedbugDemolition.com, and when the website opened with its now-familiar junky landscape, she scanned the forum titles. Nothing new; she returned to the Pictures page and stared morbidly at the photos of egg sacs, then at a series depicting the "classic bedbug bite formation"—three bites in a neat horizontal row, described as "breakfast, lunch, and dinner." There was nothing new posted from Susan's old friend 0-684-84328-5@gmail.com.

"Oh," Susan said suddenly. "Oh, shit. Right."

She hurriedly went to Gmail, holding her breath hopefully, and ran her eyes impatiently down dozens of unread subject lines, one-day sales and horoscopes and "haven't-heard-from-you" messages, until—*yes!*—there it was. In her Spam box, a reply from 0-684-84328-5@gmail.com.

She clicked the message eagerly, took a deep breath, and read:

allbedbugsarenotcreatedequaldonotcontactmeagain

"What?"

Susan squinted, yawned, and ran her finger along the screen as she puzzled out the words: *All bedbugs are not created equal do not contact me again*.

"Not created equal?" Susan whispered the words. She felt a sudden and powerful urge to stand up, slam shut the computer, and run from the house, just go sprinting off into the night in her long flannel nightgown and shower cap. Fuck Jenna. She would go to a homeless shelter.

"A homeless shelter?" she said aloud. "I don't know, those places are pretty gross. Might have, like, *bedbugs* or something."

Susan cackled, throwing her head back and bouncing peals of wicked laughter off the walls of the dark kitchen. Her lips were dry, so dry that when she grinned her bottom lip split open painfully; she flicked out her tongue, tasting the coppery tang of her blood.

On her screen, the words stared balefully out at her: *All bedbugs are not created equal do not contact me again*.

"Hmm."

Susan highlighted the strange numerical e-mail address, 0-684-84328-5@gmail.com, clicked Copy, pasted it into a Google search box, and hit Return. There were three matches—all referring back to the mystery person's postings on BedbugDemolition.com. Dead end. Susan felt a new itch at the small of her back and raked her nails at the spot.

This time she copied not the whole address, but just the numbers—0-684-84328-5.

She pasted them into the search box. Maybe it was a tracking code, for a FedEx package. Maybe it was a serial number for something. Some pest-control product, probably. *Viral marketing. Some crapola.* Maybe it was the VIN number for a car.

She pressed Enter and stared at the screen, agape.

It wasn't a tracking number. It was an ISBN code—a numerical code, assigned by a publisher to a book. As it turned out, 0-684-84328-5 was the ISBN for a book, published in 2002 by an author named Pullman Thibodaux, titled *Cimex Lectularius: The Shadow Species.*

Susan's hands began to tremble and she looked around the room; suddenly, she felt as though she could see them everywhere, the bugs, could feel them crawling under her chair, hear them hissing and clicking in the cabinets.

The Shadow Species.

The swollen bite sat at the back of her tongue, throbbing like a torturer's mark.

22.

According to the degrees covering one wall of his examination room, Dr. Lucas H. Gerstein had obtained his undergraduate degree at Brown University, proceeded to medical school at Cornell, and then done his residency in New York, at Bellevue. Dr. Gerstein was a licensed allergist and a member of the American Medical Association's Steering Committee on Pollutants and Allergens. He had a receding hairline, a large forehead lined with deep grooves, and mild grey eyes, which he now ran carefully over Susan's body.

They had chatted for a while first, and he had jotted down her answers in a thin notebook: The bugs had first appeared three weeks ago, she'd reported; yes, she'd seen the bugs—well, only one, actually, and only briefly.

"Hmm." Dr. Gerstein smiled blandly as his hands passed industriously over her body. "If you could lift your hands for me. Thanks."

Susan shivered in her paper gown. Her skin was rough and dried out as an old piece of canvas, worn and abraded. There was her wrist, of course, where the original scar, dug up and healed a million times over, was now a crosshatch of suppurated tissue. There was the spot on her left shoulder, similarly dug up, currently red rimmed and lightly oozing with pus.

Dr. Gerstein ran his gloved fingers over these marks and found more: a cluster of bites below her breasts, three or four along her right thigh, scattered bites dotting her arms. Some of the bites were small, barely visible, while others were opened and bleeding like stigmata. Some were sharp, thin, and angled, like paper cuts, others were gaping, obscene, like gashes or bullet wounds.

"Does that hurt?" the doctor asked, probing at a bite on the small of her back. His voice was thin and nasal, fussy.

"Yeah," she said, wincing. "It does." Susan's lips were dry and desiccated, and the skin of her knuckles was rough as sandpaper. When she flexed her fingers, small cracks opened up and bled fresh.

Alex sat in a hard plastic chair in the examination room, leaning forward with a worried expression. When she was pregnant, he had come to the ultrasounds, strained to hear the heartbeat, sitting awkwardly in the small examination rooms with his coat in his lap. Susan tilted her head back and exhaled. On the opposite wall was a picture of Dr. Gerstein and his homely, horse-toothed wife. As his fingertips danced over her abraded skin, they exacerbated the itch at every spot they touched.

"All right." He was pulling off the gloves. "Are there any marks I have not seen?"

"On my scalp." She pushed aside her hair, and the doctor stood up on his toes to peer at the top of her skull.

"All right."

"And—ah—there's one biting me right now."

It stung, pinched, at the sole of her foot.

"Really?" said the doctor, raising his eyebrows. "You can feel it? Right now? Bedbug bites do not typically—"

"I feel it! Look."

She turned her bare foot upward, and Alex shifted forward in the chair and furrowed his brow. Dr. Gerstein bent over the foot, took it in one delicate hand, and then looked up at Susan questioningly. There was no bug, only the faint remnant of an old bite, a pink flap of scab nearly at the point of flaking off.

"Must have . . . " Susan trailed off, cleared her throat. "Must have escaped. They're very small, you know.

"I know." He turned away. "OK, Susan, thank you."

While she dressed, Dr. Gerstein took a small pad from a pocket of his white coat and made a series of quick notes. Susan was reminded of Dana Kaufmann: the same quiet confidence and efficient motions.

Well, a lot of help she *was.*

The fresh bite on the sole of her foot itched fiercely. It took all her self-control to keep from scratching it.

*

Dr. Gerstein's diagnosis was simple and straightforward.

"I do not believe that the discomfort you are experiencing arises from bedbug bites at all," he said blandly. "It appears that you are suffering from something called Ekbom's syndrome."

Susan stared at the doctor, feeling slightly nauseous.

"Ekbom's syndrome," Alex echoed, nodding slowly, gravely intoning each syllable. "And what is that, exactly?"

"It is a condition, sometimes called delusional parasitosis, in which the sufferer comes to believe that he or she is being tormented by small insects, too small to be seen by the human eye."

At the word *delusional*, an alarm went off in Susan's mind: *oh no. oh no oh no.*

"So there aren't any bedbugs, then?" Alex said.

"Well, of course, I can't say for sure. But, I believe you said your house was examined—"

"It was."

"And—"

"Nothing."

"No," Susan interrupted. "No, no. There are bedbugs. I've *seen* them."

"You've seen—" He checked his notepad. "*One*, you stated . . ."

"Well, I've seen—" She clutched her temples, trying to remember. One on her shoulder, in the middle of the night. That disgusting little egg, on her toothbrush. In dreams, thousands of them: an army. "Two. I've seen. At least two."

Dr. Gerstein's mouth twitched up at the corners, a quick and dismissive smile. His white coat was immaculate. "I know, Susan, that you believe you have seen them."

"I believe I've seen them because I've *seen* them."

"Susan, honey, let's just listen," said Alex. "This actually makes a lot of sense."

"No, Alex. It doesn't." Of course it made sense, for Alex! If there were no bugs, if she were simply crazy, he didn't have to pay for extermination. Didn't have to move. Didn't have to be bothered at all.

"If I might interject," said Dr. Gerstein, and Susan glared at him. "Your chart indicates that you've been taking Ambien on an as-needed basis—"

"Every night, doctor," Alex interrupted. "She takes them every night."

"OK. Well, a definite correlation is hard to pinpoint, of course, but antianxiety medications can create rather extreme delusional activity. We would have—"

"Alex!" Susan looked at him, raised her arms high like tree branches. "Look at me. Look! I'm covered in bites."

"*Actually . . .* " Dr. Gerstein raised an index finger, and Susan fought the urge to bite it off. "One or two of these marks may be bites. Spider bites, perhaps, or—it's best not to speculate. But most of what you perceive as bites, given the patterning and your observable behavior, we can assume to be self-inflicted."

There was a long silence, during which every bone and sinew in Susan's body demanded that she scratch at the inflamed spot on her thigh. She sat on her hands. *My God—what if he's right,* Susan thought, the shock of it streaking across her mind fiery red, like a comet, followed by another: *I fired Marni . . . I chased her out of the house. . . .*

Susan managed, by enormous effort, to remain still, the stifled urge to scratch traveling up her arms as a series of shudders.

"Ms. Wendt, I promise you, your situation is not uncommon, and it is entirely treatable. Beginning with antihistamines and corticosteroids, just to get the swelling and itching under control. And, most important, a drug called Olanzapine, which will help your mind to understand what is really there, and what is not."

Susan nodded mutely and slid off the examination table, her head buzzing. As she dressed, she heard Alex and the doctor discussing her in low tones, as though she were a child: the doctor murmuring *hmm,* Alex asking questions in his hushed, all-business voice.

"And what can we do next . . . is she in any immediate danger . . ."

"No . . . not at all."

"She's a very strong person, just in general, that's what's so distressing . . ."

"I definitely get that. . . ."

As she tugged her shirt down over her head, Susan saw the doctor shake Alex's hand reassuringly.

"She's fine. Once she starts on the Olanzapine, the situation should begin to improve."

*

Emma, as instructed, had sat in the waiting room with Mr. Boogle, flipping through picture books. "Bye, sweetheart," sang the nurse's aide Alex had paid five bucks to keep an eye on her, and Emma grinned at her.

"Her name is Shirley," Emma announced. "She lives in Queens! Have I ever been to Queens?"

"Not yet," said Alex. "Maybe one day." The three of them proceeded slowly down Clinton Street, Alex talking the whole time, low and gentle. "We're going to get you home, we're going to get you in bed. Slip on those fuzzy slippers of yours—whatever happened to those? The ones with the mice heads?"

"I don't know." Susan smiled, thinking *I did see them, though. I saw them. I felt them.* Snaking her fingers up inside her coat sleeve, scratching furtively at her wrist. *Didn't I?*

"You know what I'm going to do? I'm going to make you soup. Chicken soup!"

"Oh! Can I put in the noodles?" asked Emma, tilting her head back in the stroller excitedly.

"Of course."

"Alex, no."

"What do you mean, no? You don't like soup all of a sudden?"

"First of all, I don't have the flu, remember? I have the crazies."

"Susan."

"What about the Tiffany job, Alex?"

"Vic will be perfectly fine." But he looked at his watch, exhaled through his teeth.

"Vic will *not* be fine."

They were at the entrance to the N/R train. Alex looked her up and down, assessing. She drew herself up straight and looked into his eyes, brushed him on the cheek with her fingertips. "You go do your thing. Me and the Emster are gonna swing by the drugstore to get this—what did he call it—marzipan."

"Olanzapine."

"That's what I said."

Alex threw an arm around her, drew her in for a hug. "If you need *anything*. . . ."

She hugged him back. "Go make some money, darling."

*

After Alex had descended into the subway, Emma wriggled around in the stroller again and peered excitedly up at Susan. "Are we going to the drugstore that has the sunglasses? Can I get a pair of Barbie sunglasses?"

"Sure, baby. But first we have to stop by the library."

23.

At first glance, *Cimex Lectularius: The Shadow Species* did not look like the answer to Susan's prayers. The book, when she finally found it in the third-floor stacks of the Brooklyn Public Library's main branch, on Grand Army Plaza, was nestled between a fat volume on spider crabs and the charmingly titled *Encyclopedia of Intestinal Parasites*. *The Shadow Species* was a slim and unimpressive hardcover, with no dust jacket and a blank, unprinted gray cover. It reminded Susan of books she'd hated in college, theoretical works with titles like *An Interpretational Aesthetics of Representational Art,* written in dense, indecipherable text. Holding *The Shadow Species* up to the flickering fluorescent library light, Susan felt a surge of disappointment.

Come on, Sue, she chastised herself, settling down across from Emma at the big table where the girl was diligently working her way through a *Wonder Pets* activity book. *What were you expecting? Golden pages? Magic sparks flying from the corners?*

Susan flipped halfheartedly through the three blank pages at the beginning of the book, feeling the dog-eared corners crumble under her fingertips. On the title page, besides the author's name (the name Pullman Thibodaux conjured for Susan a bearded British eccentric, puffing on his pipe at a meeting of the Royal Society of Explorers), she found the year of publication, 2002, and the name of the publisher,

Kastl & DuBose.

Susan asked herself again what exactly she'd been expecting, and again she had no answer. Emma giggled and held up a piece of construction paper. "Mama, look! I drew *you!*"

Susan glanced at the exuberant scribble-scrabble. "Nice work, kiddo," she said, and looked at her watch.

I'll read for ten minutes. Then we'll go get the stupid prescription.

*

The first chapter of *Cimex Lectularius: The Shadow Species* bore the bland, uninspiring title "Anatomy, Physiology, Habitat," and the text that followed was every bit as lifeless: dry and academic all the way, seemingly intended for a purely scientific audience.

> *Cimex lectularius*, as distinct from *Cimex hemipterus* or *Cimex pilosellus*, is the most numerous of the several species of the order Hemiptera, family Cimicidae. *C. lectularius* is a hematophagous nocturnal insect notable for nonfunctioning wing pads and a beaklike dual mouth proboscis. Not unusually among its fellow invertebrates, *C. lectularius* reproduces by means of traumatic insemination: as the female lacks a vaginal opening, the male pierces the female's abdomen and injects seminal fluid directly in the body cavity.

"Ugh," Susan grunted.

"What, Mama?"

"Nothing, bear. You're doing great."

"I know!" Emma waggled her eyebrows like a pint-sized Groucho Marx and bent back over her coloring. Susan's watch told her that it was 11:17, and the ten minutes she'd allotted herself had passed five minutes ago. She flipped forward and discovered that the first chapter of *Cimex Lectularius: The Shadow Species* concluded with an annotated line drawing of a bedbug: six thin legs and two antennae arranged symmetrically around the squat serrated husk of a body. The drawing made Susan's entire body hot with itches, and she hunched forward at her seat and scratched wildly, like a dog.

Five more minutes, she thought, steadying herself. *Five more minutes.*

*

Susan stared at the title of the next chapter for a few seconds before fully registering the sly, oddly unsettling play on words.

Chapter Two: Badbugs.

This bit of mild cleverness introduced a distinct shift in the prose style of *The Shadow Species*. Pullman Thibodaux, apparently finished with the detailed biological survey of his subject, now proceeded to what he called "a brief cultural history of *C. lectularius.*" In a more sprightly and conversational tone, he related how bedbugs are mentioned in two plays by Aristophanes, and then—in a series of offset text blocks—detailed their appearances in the works of Anton Chekhov and George Orwell. On the next page, the bedbug illustration from the end of Chapter One appeared again, slightly bigger this time, and again Susan was overcome by it, convulsed in a feverish spasm of scratching.

"And now we come to the crux of the matter," she read, when she had recovered. "Where we turn from the realm of fiction to that of nonfiction; from story to history."

She leaned forward, licking her dry chapped lips, and turned the page.

In the histories of Livy we find one Arobolus, a cousin by marriage to the emperor Tiberius, whose wife was cursed by a blight of bedbugs. Arobolus, far from being sympathetic, claimed he had caused the gods to curse his wife in this way, as punishment for allowing herself to be seduced by an official in the Praetorian Guard. The story ends poorly not only for the wife—who was eaten alive in her bed—but also for the prideful Arobolus, whose home is plagued thereafter by the insects, and who is ultimately driven mad by their unceasing torments.

Susan licked her lips again, peeled a crust of dried skin from the corner of her mouth. Thibodaux related more stories in a similar vein: one from the Han dynasty of ancient China, one set among the Ibo people of precolonial Nigeria. One story, from Puritan Massachusetts, involved a minister named Samuel Hopegood, who threw himself into the Charles River, believing himself "bedeviled" after a particularly nasty bedbug infestation. As these stories unspooled, Susan scratched unceasingly at her neck with the cap of a ballpoint pen, until she felt the skin split open, and the pen cap sink beneath the skin.

The final section of Chapter Two was subheaded with a single question, bolded and underlined: **AND WHY?**

Why this epic fascination with such a minor irritant?

Why should the presence of *C. lectularius* in our homes and in our beds inspire such revulsion, even to the point of insanity?

Why do we shake out the sheets, why crawl the floors of our bedrooms, hunting like dogs?

Why such hatred for fundamentally harmless pests—these tiny, non-disease-carrying, functionally invisible insects?

Susan nodded, murmuring, "Yes, yes, yes," until—when she read the next paragraph—she froze, grew still and silent. The forefinger that had been tracing the words trembled above the page.

Because it is not bedbugs that we are frightened of at all.

There is another species, a shadow species, a bedbug worse than bedbugs.

C. lectularius, for all its scuttling in bed sheets and hiding in darkness, is the species we know of, that we can understand, that we can name and track and capture and kill. But our irrational hatred and fear of C. lectularius is but an unconscious manifestation of our instinctive, and absolutely rational, hatred and fear of its sinister cousin.

This shadow species is related to C. lectularius, closely related, in the way that men and chimpanzees are related—or, more aptly, in the way that men and angels are related. Or men and demons.

I am not a scientist and cannot give the shadow species its

name. *Cimex nefarious*, perhaps? *Cimex daemonicus*?

I call them badbugs.

Susan ran her fingers down the side of her face and felt the sharp sting of her ragged nails cutting like razors into her cheeks. This was all so ridiculous. So impossible. So awful.

Bedbugs hide under mattresses and in the corners of door-frames; badbugs hide in the crevices of human history, in the instants between seconds, in the synapses between thoughts. When bedbugs latch on, they feast on blood for ten minutes and fall away; badbugs feast not only on blood, but on body and soul. And when they latch on, they feast forever.

Susan read this last paragraph again, staring at the words "body and soul" until they seemed to lift off the page and spin around before her eyes. She tried to remember: When had she read, or heard, those words before? That same cryptic phrase—*body and soul*—*not only on blood, but on body and soul?*

She snapped the book shut and looked straight ahead, her dead eyes locked on a framed antique map captioned "BREUKELEN: 1679." Her pulse rang in her temples. A shrill and furious interior voice demanded of Susan that she close the book, stick it back on the shelf, consign it to the obscurity where it belonged.

This is all bullshit, insisted this voice. *There's no way—*

Susan's fingers gripped the edges of the table. The map of old Brooklyn swam before her eyes. Call it bullshit, but she had seen that horrifying portrait of Jessica Spender, her face mutilated, her eyes wide with terror. She had felt the bites of bugs that then disappeared, unseen, leaving no trace, determined to drive her mad. Susan's body rattled. Her head throbbed. Something was buzzing. Her phone—her phone, in her pocketbook. Was vibrating. She dug it out, looked at the screen. It was Alex.

badbugs feast not only on blood—

"Hello?" Susan coughed, cleared her throat. Her mouth felt like it was coated in dust. The bite in the back of her throat throbbed. "Hey, Al."

not only on blood—

"Hey, babe. Just checking in. How you doing?"

"Oh. Great. Yeah. Doing great."

on body and soul—

"Did you pick up the prescription?"

"What?" *The prescription? Oh, right.* "Yeah. Sure did."

"Good. So, I was thinking, for dinner—"

body and soul—

"Actually, Al, I can't talk right now." She fingered the pages, rubbing the rough paper between thumb and forefinger. She forced her voice to take on a flowery, lilting tone. "We're visiting a preschool. I forgot I had made the appointment, so I figured why not?"

"Wow. She's still awake? Did you guys have lunch?"

"What? Yeah. Of course."

Susan glanced at her watch: 2:10. *Jesus.*

"Anyway, I think this place might be a great fit for Emma. I'll tell you about it later."

She looked across the table. Emma was slumped forward, her head buried in her folded arms, asleep with a forest green Crayola clutched limply in her little fist.

"Oh, well, that's great," said Alex. "And you got the medicine—"

Susan turned off her iPhone and then used its flat surface to soothe a fiery patch on her back, rubbing it between her shoulder blades. Then she jammed the phone in her pocket, reached across the table to pat Emma's hair, and kept reading.

*

But where do they come from? This shadow species, this race of tormenters, this species within—beneath—beyond a species? Where do they come from, and why?

Nobody knows. Even among those few of us who understand, who believe in this animal called badbugs, who have no choice but to believe—**nobody knows.**

But it is beyond doubt that there are places—anguished places—the kind of places that give rise to sleeping nightmares and waking dreams—those places we all know of and pretend to laugh about—where certain dogs will not set foot—where people do things late at night they do not understand, things they wish in the morning could be undone.

"Oh for fuck's sake *I knew*," Susan said, the words coming out in a dry rush of air, her whole body trembling. She remembered her night of wild, mesmerized painting, and even before that there were the dreams, from their first night in that house, the dreams . . .

"I knew I knew I knew . . . "

But even in these despairing places, the badbugs will come

only when invited.

Invited. Of course. As she read, Susan mumbled to herself, a despairing chant of self-accusation: "I knew I knew I knew ... "

Someone has to commit the act, think the thought that throws open the door to the darkness. Someone has to give off the unholy heat and light that draws forth the badbugs from the shadows. For as bedbugs are drawn to heat and carbon dioxide, badbugs are drawn to the hot stink of evil.

Susan struggled for air, heaving a series of thick breaths as she turned the page.

And now there is only one question left: How to get rid of them?

Unfortunately, there is only one way to remove the blight.

There is only one way.

What Susan read next made her whole body shake violently. She scratched at her scalp, tugging painfully at the roots of her hair. She picked at the scabs and welts that dotted her body. She gnawed at her already ravaged nails, working down the tips of fingers, down to the knuckles, which she chewed at like an animal, sucking and biting until the skin stretched over the joint split, and she tasted blood on her tongue.

She read it one more time, the short, brutal paragraph, and buried her face in her hands. "Oh, God," whispered Susan Wendt. "Oh, no."

*

"Mama? Hey, Mama-jamma?"

The sound was small and high pitched, an irritating buzz, a fly coming closer and closer. Susan kept her eyes on the pages, head bowed to the book, her hands pressed to her ears. There was only one page left, a brief and mournful postscript, and Susan read it with tears in her eyes.

> I am not a scientist, or an exterminator, or any kind of demonologist or spiritualist. All of my knowledge has been gained the hard way. If you have found this book bizarre and impossible to believe, then I pray you never have occasion to reconsider that opinion.

"Hey, Mama?"

> But if you think it's true, then for God's sake pity me. And if you *know* it's true, then it is I who pities you.

"*Mama?*"

Susan closed her eyes, slapped her palm down on the table. "*What*, Em?"

Emma stared back, startled, her eyes wide and trembling with tears; over her shoulder, Susan saw the fat librarian behind the reference desk look up and scowl. Susan must have spoken louder than she intended.

"I'm hungry, Mama."

Susan's head was pounding; her eyes burned behind their lids.

"Sorry, hon. I just . . ." Susan coughed into her fist. She closed the book. That was the end. "OK, boo-boo. OK, let's go."

*

Twenty minutes later, they were back on the subway, and Susan's whole body was trembling, her mind reeling from all she had read. Her back itched; her cheeks itched; the back of her neck itched vividly, like it was swarmed with mosquitoes or biting flies. As the train made its rumbling way from Grand Army Plaza to Bergen Street toward home, Susan noticed that all the people in the seats around them—giggly, flirty high school students, a couple of elderly retirees, a hard-faced white man with his suitcase on the seat beside him— were staring at her. No doubt about it: they could *tell*. They were watching her, shifting away from her, whispering to one another, hor- rified by what was crawling over her flesh. Susan ducked her head and looked around furtively with hot, resentful eyes. Emma, slumped be- side her in a hungry and exhausted daze, gazed up at her mom.

"Mama? Are you worried about the buggies, Mama?"

"A little bit, honey. Just a little bit."

Emma bit at her pretty red lips. "Are the buggies going to hurt me?"

"No. No, no, no." She squeezed the girl to her lap. "I promise."

The promise was like ash in her mouth. How could she prom- ise that? She let go of Emma's hand, thinking that with every touch, every loving gesture, she provided a bridge by which the monsters were jumping from her flesh onto her daughter's. The things she had read in the book were a mad jumble in her mind. The bugs were not her imagination, not the symptom of some psychiatric illness or hallucination. Something terrible had happened to her—was still happening. The bedbugs were more than bedbugs, they weren't going anywhere, and they could not be escaped.

The 2 train rolled to a stop at Clark Street, the doors swooshed open, and Susan and her daughter got off.

24.

The rest of that day, the bugs would not let Susan be.

She went through the motions of the afternoon like a robot, her body enacting the familiar movements: unclip Emma from the stroller, heave her up the stairs and through the door, prepare lunch, feed lunch, put her down for nap. When Emma woke up, Susan mustered the wherewithal to play a couple rounds of Candy Land.

Meanwhile the bugs were busy, busy, busy, flickering in the corner of Susan's eyes, dancing across her knuckles, alighting on and off the back of her neck. Susan could feel them thick in the air around her, and she caught occasional whiffs of their tell-tale scent—a musty, too-sweet stink of raspberries and coriander. But when Susan looked up from Candy Land, or from the counter where she was making coffee and preparing lunch—when she turned her eyes directly upon the bedbugs—*the badbugs, badbugs, bad bad bad*—that she knew were there—she knew they were there—when she looked closer at the cluster writhing on the countertop, or at the line marching up the side of the trash can—they would transform under her gaze into specks of dirt, or twists of fabric, or nothing . . . just, nothing at all.

"Your turn, honey," Susan murmured, setting her yellow plastic man on a blue rectangle, and rubbed her eyes with her knuckles until bright red spots danced across the back of the lids.

Alex came home a half hour earlier than his usual 6:30, acting as though not a thing were amiss in their charming little life. He was chatty and cheerful, brimming with positive news about GemFlex. The Tiffany shoot, in contrast to the Cartier debacle of last month, had gone off without a hitch. ("You were absolutely right, by the way," Alex reported with a grin. "Vic would have been lost without me.") What's more, there had been a flurry of freshly signed clients, a big uptick in receipts going into the year's end. But even as Alex prattled on, Susan could smell his nervousness, could feel his tentative movements; he was handling her with kid gloves, eyeing her anxiously, checking to see if Dr. Gerstein's prescription had begun to take effect. To see if, in the doctor's hideously condescending phrase, "the situation had begun to improve."

Sorry, pally, Susan thought grimly as she walked slowly down the stairs from putting Emma to bed. *The situation has not improved.*

She had decided that, over dinner, she would make her husband understand that precisely the opposite was true: the situation was much, much worse. Worse than Susan had ever imagined.

*

"You're not going to like what I have to say. But I need you to listen, and to try to understand."

Alex looked up from his plate, a spot of salad dressing on his chin, and examined Susan through the flowers that sat in a vase in the center of the kitchen table. It was a gaudy autumnal bouquet he'd brought home from Trader Joe's, flushed with russet and orange, but all Susan could see in it were hiding places. She knew that the bugs were slipping up and down the stems, paddling in the stale water at the bottom of the vase. Susan hadn't touched her salad. She sipped from a cup of coffee, the last of the pot she'd brewed hours ago, bitter, thick and gritty with sediment.

It was Friday November 5, at 8:40 p.m. The Wendts had been living at 56 Cranberry Street for fifty-four days.

"Go ahead," Alex said gently. "I'm listening."

Susan took a breath and pushed her fingers with difficulty through her knotted, greasy hair. To have even a chance of getting Alex on her side, Susan knew, she needed to make all this insanity sound as nice and not-insane as she could. As *normal* as she could.

"OK, so, I found this book."

"OK . . ."

She told Alex about *Cimex Lectularius: The Shadow Species*, making it sound basically like an entomological textbook, very scientific, very dry and serious.

"The bottom line is, we somehow got these bedbugs," she continued, while Alex sat stone faced on the other side of the table. "This particular *strain* of bedbugs, you might say. And, basically, they're not going away."

"So." Alex took off his glasses and exhaled deeply. "This is about moving again."

"No. It's not above moving. God, I wish it were. Something very bad happened in this house. I think it has to do with the old tenants, with Jack and Jessica Spender."

"What are you talking about?"

"Something *happened*. Something—something awful. And moving won't help. They've got me now, Alex. They've got me."

"Susan?"

She waved away his hand, gritted her teeth, ordered herself to keep it together. The tingling itch made itself known on her inner thigh, and she fought a need to scratch.

"There's only one way to end the *curse*, you see."

Alex's eyes narrowed. "Did you say a curse?"

Well, Susan thought. *So much for keeping it nice and not-insane.*

"Yes, Alex. This house is cursed. The book uses the word "blighted," but it's the same difference. And the thing is, now I've ... I've got it somehow. I've got the blight. I think I know how to end it, but it's ... " Her voice descended into a rasping whisper. "I don't know if I can do it."

Susan looked searchingly into her husband's eyes, looking for some glint of understanding, of empathy. They had met eight years ago and had been married for five. They had honeymooned in Finland, after putting sixteen countries in a hat and both swearing to abide by whichever came out first. Finland had been amazing, a wonderland of saunas and smoked fish and dreamlike bogs.

Please, just let him—let him understand. Let him try to understand.

Alex's mouth opened slightly, and then, after a moment, he said, "Did you pick up the Olanzapine prescription?'"

Susan squeezed her eyes shut and groaned, and in the silence that followed, she heard it, loud and vivid: a terrible deep hissing, a sibilant thrum in the back of her worn-out brain pan. The badbugs were laughing, a hideous insectine laughter, the devil's own gleeful laughter. They were all around her now, in their colonies, in their swarms, massed and ready to strike ... beneath the floorboards, under the sink, in the closets and the mattresses. Waiting. Susan gave in to the need to scratch, dove her hand into her lap and worked urgently at the fiery itches on her thighs.

"No, Alex, I didn't pick up the prescription."

"Why not?"

"Why—" Susan interrupted herself with a dry and rattling cough and shook her head. She raised her hands from her lap to drag her nails across her prickly scalp, and dry white pieces of skin tumbled onto the table. Alex looked down at the floor.

"Susan, please," he murmured, and Susan thought, *This is useless. Useless* . . . "The medicine—"

"Alex, we are in serious danger. I am in danger. Can you understand that?"

Alex spoke slowly, choosing his words carefully. "I understand that you *believe* that you are in danger." He reached across the table and took her rough, twitching hands in his own. "I am going to help you through this. You have an illness, baby. You're sick."

She jerked her hands away. "I'm not."

"The landlord said we do not have bedbugs. The doctor said we do not have bedbugs. The *bedbug exterminator,* the amazing Kaufstein, the exterminator to the stars—I'm quoting now—"

"I know what you're doing."

"OK, well, *she* said we do not have bedbugs." Alex's voice was hardening, growing louder, and he shook his head as he spoke. "Look, I am not upset with you. I'm not. But you have a problem. And you have to deal with it."

Alex rose from the table. His big hands were balled into fists, the fists pressed into his sides. Susan got up, too, and stared defiantly into his eyes. "I don't care what anybody says. We have bad—we have bedbugs, and they are not going away. "

Alex stepped backward, closed his eyes, and said nothing.

"I need you, Alex! I need your help." She put her hands on his shoulders, peering up at him until he opened his eyes. "I need you to believe me."

"Oh, Susan." He roped his arms around her, gathered her into his chest, and rested his chin on her head. "Oh, baby. The doctor said—"

"Please, Alex . . . " She spoke into his chest. Tears streamed down her cheeks. "Please . . . "

"—the doctor specifically said that a symptom of this, this Ekbom's syndrome, can be a belief that the insects are persecuting you, and you alone. He said that rejecting the reality of the condition can itself be a symptom of the condition."

Susan pulled away from him, scowling. "That makes no sense."

"Well, it makes a lot more sense than supernatural monster bed-bugs."

Susan didn't know what else to say. A miserable silence welled up in the room between them. Alex leaned against the doorframe, held his face in his hands, and let out a low grunt of frustration. Susan paced between the kitchen table and the stove, her mind pinwheeling: she thought of waiting until tomorrow morning, when Alex took Emma to ballet, and setting the building on fire. She contemplated following the example of the late, great Howard Scharfstein, wandering down to that creepy basement and blowing her brains out.

At some point, Alex turned, shook his head, and slipped out of the room. As Susan watched him go, one of the tiles of the pressed-tin ceiling fell abruptly from its place and clattered noisily onto the wooden floorboards just behind her. Susan wheeled around and gaped at the ceiling. The square of plaster now exposed was like the space under a rock that's been turned over, writhing with dozens and dozens of tiny brown and black bugs. As Susan watched wide-eyed, the badbugs began to fall, dropping in uneven, weightless rows to the kitchen floor, where they landed like paratroopers, scurrying off to the corners, alone, in pairs or little groups.

Susan watched, frozen, as the bugs ran off in all directions, and then she heard it: a cheery knock from the front door.

"Susan? Yoo-hoo? So sorry to bother you, dear."

25.

Andrea Scharfstein, as it turned out, was having some trouble with her phone.

"I am so sorry to be a pain in the tush, Suze, but I am supposed to talk to my sister Nan at ten, which means seven o' clock in Portland. If she doesn't hear from me right on the dot, she gets nervous. You know how old ladies are."

She gave Susan one of her broad, teasing winks, slouching with theatrical casualness against the doorframe.

"Oh," said Susan.

"Anyhoo, you said if I was ever having trouble with this silly thing . . . " Andrea sighed, holding up the phone with a playfully apologetic smile. "So, but I'm barging in. How are *you*, kiddo?"

The absurdity of the question, considering Susan's surreal and terrifying circumstances, rendered her speechless for a moment. She thought of the bugs on her kitchen floor, scattering in all directions from the fallen ceiling tile, like soldiers preparing for an ambush. She thought of bugs in the hall closet, just behind her, slipping in and out of coat pockets. Bugs wreathing the air shaft, clinging to the cracks.

"Oh, I'm just fine, thanks," she said tonelessly. "Just fine."

"So, can you take a look at the thing? I just hate to think of old

Nan fretting away, thinking I've been crushed under an armoire or something."

"Sure. You bet."

Andrea was wearing lavender leggings, a long flowing night-gown, and an old-fashioned robe, tied loosely with a sash. Her hair was piled atop her head, in curlers. *I am under assault from an army of demonic insects,* Susan thought, the notion drifting untethered through the buzzing fog of her mind, *and Mrs. Roper is here for tech support.*

"Oh, you're a lifesaver, dear. Absolutely a lifesaver." She stepped past Susan, toward the kitchen, and the front door closed behind her. "Shall I put up the kettle for us?"

*

Susan sat at the kitchen table with her hands folded in front of her while Andrea busied herself in the kitchen, pulling open draw-ers, rummaging for teabags, sugar, spoons. The aggressive normalcy of the situation began, against all odds, to steady Susan's nerves: it seemed impossible that these two worlds could exist simultaneously, that a cheerful old woman could be fixing a pot of tea in the same apartment—in the same *universe*—where Susan was being tormented by a shadow species sent from some circle of hell. Andrea did not seem to notice the ceiling fragment, still lying dead center on the kitchen floor, or else she just chose not to mention it, stepping around or over it as she bustled about in her absurd robe and sash.

"Handsome hubby's asleep?"

"What? Oh—yes," Susan said.

"I used to be the same way. Howard would tuck himself in at nine o'clock, or go up to read his mysteries, and I'd wander about the house for another hour or two. Liked the 'alone time,' I suppose. No shortage of that now."

"Hmm," said Susan, and then she squinted at Andrea's phone, a cheap Samsung clamshell, five or six years old, lying on the kitchen table next to her own shiny pink-cased iPhone. "So, what exactly is the issue?"

"Well, it won't *do* anything, that's all! I'm sure I put it on some daffy setting or something, but I'll be darned if I can undo it."

Susan poked at the power button. "It's got no battery, that's all. No power. When did you last charge it?"

"It's been charging all day."

"And are you sure the outlet is working?"

"The . . . " Andrea tilted her head back, whacked herself dramatically on the forehead with the heel of her hand. "My goodness, now that you mention it, my hair dryer hasn't been working *either*, and I keep that on the same plug."

Susan slid the dead phone across the table and managed a tight smile.

"I was actually going to bring the dryer down also, but I thought, 'Well, for heaven's sake, Susan is a busy person, she's not your own personal Maytag repairman.' Even just the phone seemed enough of an intrusion . . . oops, there's the kettle!"

*

Andrea had a free hand with the sugar, but Susan sipped the tea gratefully, enjoying the sensation of sweet burn on her throat. The older woman remained standing, leaning back against the counter with her stick arms crossed, peering at Susan over the rims of her reading glasses while they drank their tea.

"All right, young lady," she said at last, playfully stern. "You want to tell me exactly what's going on here?"

Susan looked up.

"Because I'm going to be honest with you, hon. You don't look so hot."

Andrea leveled Susan with a caring, motherly gaze. "You can tell me, sweetheart. What are landladies for? Is it—" She angled her chin upward, toward the bedroom, and brought her voice down to a low and raspy voice. "Is it Alex?"

"No. No, not exactly."

Susan felt the rising tide of anxiety and desperation welling up from her stomach, filling her chest. She didn't think she could bear telling the whole story to Andrea, to have one more person tell her how crazy she was being. But it was too late; she put her head down on the table and moaned long and loud.

"Oh, God, Andrea. Oh, God, oh, God."

The older woman rushed over, her slippers shushing across the hardwood, and sat down beside her. "Susan, Susan, Susan." Andrea patted her on the shoulder, laid her head across her back, like a mother bird. "My goodness, what's happened?"

Susan raised her head from the table, wiping tears from her eyes with the rough, rutted backs of her hands. "It's bedbugs, Andrea. This apartment has bedbugs, after all."

"Oh, no!" Andrea said, her hand flying to her mouth. She looked around anxiously. "But I thought the exterminator, that young lady, said you were clear."

"She did—" Susan stopped to blow her nose in a napkin. "She said so, but unfortunately she was wrong. Just . . . she was wrong."

A tiny bedbug appeared on the arm of Andrea's chair. As Susan watched in mute horror, the insect skittered onto Andrea's shirt sleeve and down the withered line of her arm.

"Well, you know, Susan," Andrea was saying, "If it's necessary, I will of course pay for an exterminator."

"Andrea . . . "

"What, dear?"

The bedbug—*badbug,* Susan reminded herself with a shudder, *bad bad bad*—was advancing toward the wet pink sore that glistened on Andrea's forearm. The bug would slip into it, swim around in that pool of exposed blood. Susan's hand jerked forward, slapped at the bug. Andrea looked up, stunned at the sudden violence.

"Sorry—there was—"

Susan turned over her hand. Nothing. No broken husk, no smear of brown and red. It had escaped. *Oh, God. Oh, dear God, don't let me be crazy.* She dug her ragged, clawlike fingernails into her palms and began a desperate internal incantation: *I am not—I am not crazy. I am not crazy.* Susan looked at the floor, and the fallen ceiling tile was still there; as she watched, a bug, small and brown like a lentil, slipped out from underneath it and darted to the pantry.

"Now, listen," Andrea said. "Because this is very simple. We are going to call back that lady who came. No, that's silly. We are going to call someone new. I am sure that in Howard's Rolodex there are a zillion exterminators."

Susan shook her head, still working at the insides of her palms, feeling blood well up where she had broken through the flesh. She knew what would happen if Dana Kaufmann came back, or anyone else: they would look everywhere, turn the apartment upside down, and find nothing.

The bugs were for Susan—for Susan alone. Body and soul.

She moaned again and trailed out into a kind of desperate hiss. Andrea made a soft sympathetic exhale, brought her chair closer to Susan's, and draped one thin bony arm over her shoulders.

"What does Alex think?"

Susan shook her head and gulped tea, wishing it were coffee. Her eyes ached, her brain thumped inside her skull.

"Alex is not being that helpful."

"Men," Andrea barked. "Men and their secrets."

Susan looked up, struck by the change in Andrea's voice. The thin comedienne's growl had transformed in that one sentence, dropped into a deep, angry rasp: "With their *hiding*. And their *lying*. And never there when you need them to be. Never, never."

As she spoke Andrea looked off into the distance, out the windows above the stove at the streetlights punctuating the darkness beyond, and Susan examined her face. There was a coldness behind her eyes, a steely sadness that Susan had never seen before: the old lady was reliving some memory, something painful and raw. Susan studied her, rubbing together her bloodied palms.

"Andrea?"

"Yes, kiddo?"

It was as if a hypnotist had snapped his fingers: the light came back into Andrea's eyes, and with a smile she turned her attention back to Susan. "Here's what we'll do. If you're worried, we'll just get you the heck out of here, that's all. Right now. Tonight."

"It won't work."

"What do you mean it won't work?" Andrea was on her feet, all business, retying her robe with brisk movements. "Just for a couple nights, you and the whole gang, a nice hotel. On my dime, of course.

Heck, maybe I'll come with you. The Marriott, right here on Adams
Street, isn't a bad hotel, all things considered, though of course I
haven't stayed there in years. A nice hotel, doesn't that sound just the
thing, Susan?"

Hotel.

As soon as Andrea said it, the word clanged like a bell in Susan's
mind. Rang again each time she repeated it.

Hotel.

Hotel.

Hotel.

Susan stared at the kitchen table, boring into it with her eyes,
picturing the badbugs working through the swirls in the wood, just
below the surface. And her mind worked at that word—*hotel*—like a
tongue works at a dead tooth.

Hotel.

With their hiding. *And their* lying.

The matchbook in Alex's pocket.

The matchbook from the Mandarin Oriental Hotel.

Someone has to commit the act

Susan had *laughed* at herself for being so silly. Ever to think that
her husband would do such a thing, would go out to some hotel . . .

that throws open the door to the darkness.

But, oh, he had been out so late, hadn't he? Two in the morning.
That night, that Friday night, just after they moved to Brooklyn. She
had finally started painting again, and she'd slipped into some bizarre
unconscious state and added violence into her art, covered poor Jessica Spender with bedbug bites. Meanwhile, where was handsome
hubby? Why, just over at the Mandarin Oriental Hotel, and not alone
. . . and then she had laughed at herself for being such a shrew, a jeal-

ous little wifey. . . .

Someone has to commit the act, think the thought that throws open the door to the darkness.

The Mandarin Oriental Hotel. And then—the next morning—*the next morning*—a spot of blood on her pillow.

For as bedbugs are drawn to heat and carbon dioxide, badbugs are drawn to the hot stink of evil.

"Susan?"

Andrea was waving her hands in front of Susan's eyes, snapping her fingers. Susan stood abruptly, and the legs of her chair scraped loudly on the kitchen floor.

"Andrea, it's time for you to go downstairs and call your sister, I think."

"Yes. But—"

"Nan will be worried sick, Andrea. Just worried to death."

She grabbed the two teacups by their handles and tossed them in the sink, moving quickly, feeling a kind of delirious lightness. She plucked the phones off the kitchen table, handed Andrea's to her and stuck her own in her pocket. "Susan?"

She led Andrea by the elbow, down the hallway and to the door.

"Glad to help. Good night, Andrea."

Susan stood with her hand on the doorknob, listening to the muffled patter as Andrea scurried down the steps. *Cimex Lectularius: The Shadow Species* had said in no certain terms how the curse could be undone, how the badbugs could be sent back to the other side.

And now there is only one question left: How to get rid of them?

Unfortunately, there is only one way to remove the blight.

Someone invited the bugs in. Someone opened the door to the darkness.

That person must be discovered, and destroyed.

Pullman Thibodaux was unequivocal on that last point. Susan marched back to the kitchen counter, where the knife block sat thick and squat, like a gargoyle. She ran her fingers along the protruding handles, hearing Alex's voice in her head, condescending, chastising. *I've told you, save the good knives for when you really need a good knife.*

"Totally," Susan said. "You're totally right, honey." She wrapped her fingers around the heaviest handle and slid the butcher's knife free from the block.

26.

The little TV on Alex's dresser was on, as if he had intended to wait up for her and continue their conversation, but he had fallen fast asleep. He lay in a nest of pillows, his thick curly hair splayed out around his head, mouth half open, snoring gently. Susan turned off the TV and watched him sleep, the handle of the butcher knife sweating in her palm. The room was silent but for the baby monitor on the night table, emitting its steady sibilant crackle.

Susan crouched beside her husband and whispered in his ear: "Bad news, Alex. We have bedbugs."

He muttered something unintelligible, licked his lips, and turned over, presenting her with the back of his head. She whispered again, a little louder, in his other ear: "Lots and lots and lots and lots and lots of them."

He slept on.

"Dammit, Alex, wake *up.*" She smacked him on the side of the head, as hard as she could, cracking the butt of the handle on the base of his skull.

"Get *up.*"

Alex shot up into a crawling position and then fell forward again, gripping the back of his head. He flipped over, blinking, confused, the covers bunching around his torso. "Susan? Did you—what—"

He saw the knife and froze with his mouth open. His hair sprung out in all directions, a crust of drool pooled at the corner of his mouth. His eyes were brown and wide. Susan had always loved his eyes. As she held up her knife, watching him tremble, she felt a sudden sharp sting at the back of her neck: new bite. New itch.

Susan winced but did not release her grip on the knife. He had done this to her. All of the pain and confusion and misery. All of the itching. *He had done it.*

"What are you doing, Susan?"

"Why did you do it?"

"Why did I do *what?*"

She swung the knife, inexpertly. He jerked back and the blade just barely caught him, tracing a bright line of blood along the tan flesh of his forearm. Alex shrieked, high and womanish, pulled back against the headboard. Both of them stared at the long line of the cut, and then up at each other.

"What were you doing at the Mandarin Oriental Hotel the Friday night after we moved to Brooklyn?"

"What? Susan—"

"Friday, September 17. The Mandarin Oriental Hotel."

All the details were completely clear to Susan, totally available to her. Now she knew the story, of how her life had fallen to pieces, and why. Because of whom.

"I seriously don't know what you're—"

He cut himself off, midsentence, and lunged for the knife. She jumped backward, steadied herself on her back foot, and parried forward, nearly cutting him again. Alex retreated against the pillows, lifting the comforter over his chest as if it were a shield.

"Susan, I swear to God I have never been to the Mandarin

Oriental Hotel."

"Don't lie," Susan said flatly. The knife trembled in her hand. "Please, don't lie."

"You're sick, Sue. You have—"

She cut him again and did a better job of it, swinging the blade like a scythe, right across his ribs. The knife bit deep, biting into the fat layer of flesh above his heart, and she could feel the resistance of meat beneath the blade. Alex brought his arm down and then up, staring at the sticky mess in his hand.

"Oh, God. Susan—"

"Tell me the truth," she hissed.

"OK," Alex said slowly, pressing his hands against the wound, keeping his eyes on the knife, now smeared and dripping with his blood. "All right. Um . . . I did. That night, the . . . "

"The seventeenth."

"I ran into this girl. This old friend of mine."

"What's her name?"

He swallowed hard, staring at the knife.

"Uh, Theresa."

Susan scowled. "Theresa?"

"From—from college. You don't know her. She's a photographer, too, from my program. Nobody special—just this girl. "

As his confession unspooled, tears trickled down Susan's cheeks. Not because he had cheated on her, had betrayed her, had fucked some stupid girl from NYU in a hotel room. Susan was crying *because she was going to have to kill him* in order to end this terrible torment. He had drawn the badbugs to the hot stink of his evil, and she would have to sacrifice him like a pig on an altar or they would consume her.

"Susan?" He looked at her in the darkness, his eyes wide and wet with fear, his chest drooling blood around his hands. Susan felt the prickly heat of a thousand itches all over her body, felt the weight of the knife in her hand, heard it demanding action. She stepped toward the bed and was distracted by a small shifting noise over the monitor, a barely audible pop and crackle: Emma shifting, adjusting herself in sleep. Out of sheer instinct, Susan turned her head to the sound, and Alex leaped at her.

*

The next six minutes passed in a wild panting frenzy.

Alex rolled from the bed, tossing the sheets and comforter to the ground, kicking his legs into Susan's midsection. She went down hard on her ass, and Alex flung himself on top of her, wrestling her arm down, slapping at her hands, grabbing for the knife. She brought her knee up into his stomach and then cracked the knife handle into his jaw. He cried out and reared back, clutching his mouth, blood gushing between his fingers, more blood spilling from his chest. Susan slipped out from under him and hurled herself out of the bedroom.

He stumbled after her onto the landing, shouting, "Goddamn it, Susan, stop!" and then "Shit!" as his toe connected with the split in the floorboards. Susan halted, abruptly, stepping to one side just in time to let his big lumbering body chase itself past her, onto the top step. And then she was behind him, pushing him, hard, two hands in the middle of the back. Alex went tumbling down the steps, banging his head against the wall as he fell, and she chased after him, butcher's knife clutched in two hands.

When he landed at the bottom, she was towering over him, straddling his body with her legs.

"Susan. Please. Think about what you're doing. *Please.*"

She took a deep breath, bared her teeth.

"I'm sorry, Alex."

She brought the knife down, fast, like a missile whistling toward its target, right at Alex's neck, but he rolled away, kicking at her shins. She got up and followed, and they paraded slowly down the hallway: he walking backward, facing her with his hands raised, she following, one big step forward for each of his steps backward. She slashed at him, big wild uneven swings of the knife.

"Susan!"

He ducked as the knife sang just under his nose.

"Susan! Jesus, Susan, *stop!*"

They were in the living room now, passing under the archway and the ornately beautiful old sconces. In the corner of her eye Susan saw bugs crawling in and out of the teardrop-shaped light-bulbs that adorned the fixtures, bugs like sports fans crowding the bleachers.

Now Alex had his back to the wall of the living room, just to the right of the small door that led to the bonus room. Susan stepped toward him with the knife raised, and Alex grabbed her wrists and spun her around. She had a lunatic flash of memory, dancing at their wedding, *one-two-three, one-two-three.* And then it was Susan's back against the wall and he had her pinned, his chest against hers, smashing her breasts, constricting her breath, his full weight pressed across her body.

Alex flung open the door of the bonus room, grabbed Susan by the waist, and shoved her inside. He slammed the door and she grabbed at the handle, rattled it, screaming, but Alex was holding it closed. She could picture him, leaning backward with the handle in his hands, sealing her in. She banged on the door.

"Alex!"

There was a loud scraping noise—what—oh, God. The sofa. Still holding the door tightly shut with one hand, he had reached with the other for the giant heavy leather sofa, was dragging it in place to block the door, pen her in. She pounded on the door. "Alex! Don't leave me here!" The adrenalin-fueled anger in her veins was cooling rapidly, freezing into fear. She hammered the door with her fists. "Let me out, Alex."

"Susan, I'm going to take Emma somewhere safe, and I'll be back soon."

*Emma—no—*Alex wouldn't know what to pack for her, wouldn't know how to take care of her. Her girl, her daughter.

"Alex. Wait."

"I'm sorry, Susan."

"Let me out, Alex. Don't leave me here." The magnitude of what was occurring swelled up in her, like a balloon expanding in her gut. She pressed her palms against the door. "Please."

His footsteps moved out of the living room, pounded up the stairs toward the bedrooms. She tried the door again, and then leaned her forehead against it, tears cascading down her cheeks.

"Please."

Five minutes later, the footsteps were back on the stairs. She heard Alex grunt, shifting Emma's sleeping weight in his arms. Abstract, disconnected worries floated helter-skelter through her mind: Was he bringing her heavy coat? What would she have for breakfast? Where would they go?

*

    The front door closed, and after a few terrible minutes of silence, Susan rose shakily to her feet and turned to survey the room in which she was now imprisoned. The painting remained where she had left it, pinned to her easel in the corner, just beside the window. It was still covered in the bites and welts that Susan did not remember painting.

    But it was no longer a painting of Jessica Spender.

    It was a self-portrait.

    It was her.

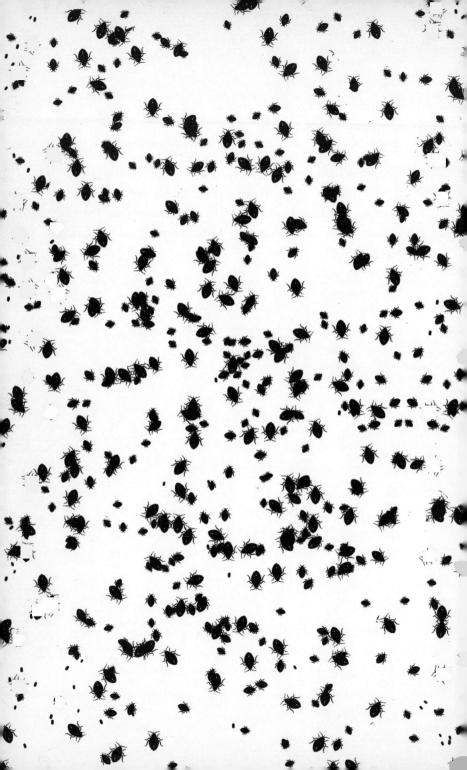

BOOK III

27.

The first of the badbugs crawled in under the door about an hour later.

It might have been less than an hour, or it might have been more. Susan wore no watch, and the moon gave no clue, hanging mute and unmoving in the window.

It was just the one bug, and it was not a big one. A stage three, Susan thought, maybe even a stage two. An eighth of an inch. Someone who was not waiting for it would never have noticed. But Susan's eyes were trained, and she *was* waiting. Now they were coming for her. Susan was sure of that.

She watched the little bug from where she sat in the far corner of the room, under the one big window, where she had first discovered the photograph of Jessica and Jack. It crawled toward her, and Susan watched it come. Her knees were drawn up in front of her, her hands laced across the kneecaps. No more hiding for Susan's friends, no more darting out when others couldn't or wouldn't see.

Now she was awake and alive and in their time, and they were coming.

The little stage three, a dark brown oval, a tiny creeping shadow in the moonlight, took a winding course across the hardwood floor, making its roundabout way to where Susan sat, waiting for it, her stomach churning with dread. A single bug. It skittered forward a foot, paused, skittered forward another half foot. Doubled back, circled around, came closer still.

No reason to hurry, the bug was saying with its easy meandering pace. *We've got you now.*

She looked at the badbug, and the badbug looked back at her.

No eyes, she told herself. Cimex lectularius *have no eyes. Six legs, two antennae, nonfunctional wing pads, and a dual tubelike proboscis . . . but no eyes.*

"But you're still looking at me, aren't you?" Susan whispered, and jumped at the sound of her own voice in the tomblike silence of the room.

Her new friend was not startled. It kept moving forward.

It's so small, Susan told herself, breathing deeply. *So small. What was this thing, this tiny insect, going to do—what could it really do to her?*

But she knew the answer. The answer she had never dared to contemplate, and now she had no choice. It was going to latch on to her and drink her blood. They had latched on to her soul, and now they had come for her body. This little bug would latch on and drink until it was full, and then another would come, and then another, as many as it took to drain her of her blood, every drop of it, until she was an empty shell, a dry rag, the empty husk of a person.

They were going to eat her alive.

The solitary badbug came within three feet, and then made a long, lazy U-turn to return to the door, and left the room.

*

Susan shook herself into action.

She stood up, flexing her arms and legs, cracking her knuckles and growling her throat clear. She walked across the room and tried the door again, rattling the handle and pushing as hard as she could, crouching down. Nothing. She backed up the eight or so paces to the far side of the bonus room and threw herself forward, slamming against the door, shoulder first, so that her whole body shook with the impact.

"Shit," Susan muttered, massaging her bruised arm.

She looked at the crack beneath the door, but no more badbugs were crawling in—not yet. She moved her eyes along the baseboard, and her glance came to rest on the spot where poor Catastrophe the cat had left his desperate scratches. Susan crouched down to trace her fingernails in the ruts, imagining the poor cat scratching madly, slowly going crazy, slowly dying as she was dying now—

Stop it, Susan told herself. *Alex will come back. He'll be back, just like he said. He's taking Emma out to his parents on Long Island, or to Vic's place on the Upper West Side, and he'll be back. Another hour. A couple hours at the most. You'll apologize. Promise to take the the Olanzapine, whatever the hell it was called.*

I can last until Alex gets back from Long Island.

*

"Help!"

Susan pounded on the door, hard, with the flat of her hand. She had been pounding for forty-five minutes, and the pad of flesh at the base of her palm was red and raw. Her voice ached from screaming.

"Andrea! Please! Help!"

She pounded more. Andrea would hear, the noise would boom through the living room, echo down the air shaft, into her bedroom and wake her. She would come up and save her.

If Alex hadn't locked the deadbolt on the front door.

If Andrea could move the sofa.

If she heard the banging.

Which, clearly, she did not.

*

When the next badbug came in under the door, Susan leaped up out of her crouch, scrabbled across the floor on hands and knees, and squashed it with her forefinger. She pressed her fingertip down on the tiny creature and pushed as hard as she could, bringing to bear the full weight of her upper body, until she was sure she felt the minute *scritch* of the creature's husk cracking from the pressure. But when she lifted her finger and held it up to the moonlight, there was no bloody red smear across the tip.

The bug was alive and at work: it had latched onto the pad of her fingertip. Sucking her blood.

"Oh, God," Susan said. She shook her hand back and forth violently, flapping it like a bird's wing to fling the thing free. It did not come loose. As it continued to eat, Susan felt a prick of pain at the spot where the bug was latched, a sharp sting in the center of her fingertip. *No more with the anesthetizing anticoagulant fluid now—the bugs had her where they wanted, and they didn't care whether she knew they were biting or not.* Susan shaped the forefinger and thumb of her other hand into a pincer and grasped at the bug, tried to pull it free of her flesh, but it dug in and would not come loose. The more she tugged, the more it hurt, an excruciating, radiating pain, like a needle wiggling in a vein.

Susan gave up and held her hand in front of her bleary eyes, watching the bug as it drank. She counted quietly to herself, ticking off the seconds, and then the minutes. One minute . . . two . . .

After a little more than twelve minutes, the thing dropped off, fell to the floor, and skittered a drunken staggering path back to the crack beneath the door. Susan turned her gaze to her finger, watched as the welt blossomed on the tip, round and red and hard.

Susan felt tired . . . so tired. The awful self-portrait hovered over her, her own terrified features glowering back at her in the grim moonlit darkness of the room.

*

When she stuck her wounded hand into her pocket, a few minutes later, she found her iPhone where she had jammed it, and she nearly laughed out loud with relief. *I've been sitting here*, Susan thought. *Sitting here like an idiot, with my phone in my pocket!* The wallpaper picture of Emma, upside down on the monkey bars, tugged at her heart. The digital display told her it was 1:45 in the morning.

She called Alex but disconnected the call after a single ring, suddenly afraid of speaking to him. What if he said he wasn't coming home? What if he refused to help her? Which, by the way, would be perfectly reasonable, considering . . .

Susan glanced down at the floor and saw two new badbugs, zipping across the floor toward her: no lazy meandering circles now, no slow and easy progress. These two were making a rapid crisscross motion as they advanced, twin fighter jets closing in on their target.

Susan texted quickly, her thumbs flying across the keyboard:

ALEX I AM SORRY PLS COME HOME I NEED U PLS

Susan hit Send just as the bugs arrived at her feet; she tried to stomp them and missed, then watched in horror as they disappeared up her pant legs. She danced, shaking her legs, but it was too late—she felt them latch on, one on her calf, the other on the tender flesh of her inner thigh. Tears filled Susan's eyes. The pain was worse this time, fiery and intense. They were taking what they wanted now, ruthlessly, and it *hurt*.

She texted Alex again, PLS PLS PLS PLS PLS, and then gave up and called him. It rang and rang.

"Hey, it's Al Wendt. Looks like I'm too busy for the likes of you. Go ahead and—"

She ended the call. More bugs were swarming in under the door, dozens of them, and she watched them advance in an uneven black line. The ones on her legs kept sucking, even as the new bites began: one under her chin and another on the small of her back, just above her ass.

Susan found Andrea Scharfstein in her contacts list, jabbed furiously at the number.

"Andrea, if you're awake—if by some chance you get this, can you call me? Or, or just come up, because—I—oh, *God* . . . "

Tiny little legs scurried up Susan's neck, danced across the delicate skin under the earlobe and into her ear. And then the sting, as the bug latched on to the membrane just inside her ear canal. Susan screamed and jammed her pinky finger into the ear, but the bug was deep inside her head, past where her finger could follow, and it was biting her, the pain was unspeakable, and she could hear it, amplified a hundredfold, the hideous *suck suck suck* as the insect drank from the tender flesh.

Susan screamed and screamed. The phone fell from her hands and she watched the console light flash brightly and go dim. There were active bites all over her body now—her legs, her ass, her crotch, her ear, above her eyelid and under her chin, points of pain throbbing red all over her skin. She hurled herself at the door of the bonus room, again and again, pounding the wooden door with her frail body, ignoring the shockwaves of pain that rocked her frame with each strike. Badbugs were pouring in under the door now, hundreds of them, a low tide welling in around her feet, snapping at her ankles like fleas. Susan backed away from the door, retreated into the far corner of the room, sank to the ground, and threw her hands up over her face.

She had to keep fighting, had to somehow escape . . . where had her phone gone, where had she dropped it . . . but there were so many of them . . . and she was so terribly tired . . .

So tired . . .

*

In her dream Susan simply stood up and shook the badbugs free, like a rain-soaked dog shaking itself dry. She turned to the windowsill and saw him, as clear as crystal in the moonlight—*Louis!* Good old Louis, right outside, striding across the concrete slabs of the garden like a modern Colossus, squinting up at the window, mouthing her name.

"Susan?"

"Louis!"

She cried his name, pounding on the windowpanes, and he raised both hands in greeting. He had come to check on her. He was worried about her, and he'd come to check in. *Good old Louis!*

She screamed his name. *"Louis!"*

The moonlight glinted off the cheap plastic frames of his glasses. He held up a finger, to say "just one second," and took another step toward the house. And then Andrea appeared behind him, holding a long claw-hammer. Susan screamed, *"No!!"* and Louis furrowed his brow, just before Andrea swung the hammer high above her head and brought it down squarely on the back of Louis's skull. He buckled and collapsed, blood erupting from the top of his head, and all around him hammers rained from the sky, bloody hammers spiraling down, burying themselves in the earth . . . and then babies, bloody babies buckled in their strollers, tumbling out of the night.

Andrea walked through them like a ghost slipping between raindrops, back toward the house.

*

Susan woke up, screaming, and immediately heard the sound of wood scraping on wood.

The sofa. Someone was moving the sofa.

Susan blinked. The room was full of sunlight. There was a row of bugs on her forearm, and there was one on her face, she could feel it on her cheek, biting, right now, she could feel it . . .

But—*oh, God, oh, God, thank God*—someone was moving the sofa.

"Alex!" she called, or tried to call, but her voice came out as a gritty dry rattle. "Alex?"

"No, ma'am."

As soon as Dana Kaufmann opened the door her mouth dropped open. The exterminator's voice emerged as a cold dead whisper: "Holy *crap*."

28.

"You see them?" whispered Susan desperately from where she lay in a heap in the far corner of the room. The bug currently sucking blood from her face unlatched, descended onto her stomach, and skittered away. Bugs meandered across her arms and legs; bugs threaded in and out of her eyebrows; bugs swarmed in clumps and swirls across the floorboards, in patches all over the room. "You really see them?

Dana Kaufmann stepped slowly into the bonus room, her big brown work boots crunching on patches of bugs. The badbugs, made wild by her presence, dashed in frenzied patterns around and past her footsteps as she made her way to Susan, bent over, and extended her hand.

"I see them," said Dana Kaufmann. Now that her initial shock had worn off, Kaufmann sounded like Susan remembered: gruff, stoic, and reassuring. "I do, Ms. Wendt. I see them all."

*

"What I need you to understand, first and foremost, Ms. Wendt, is that there are no pests I cannot kill. None. Do you understand?"

Susan was sitting cross-legged on the kitchen table in her bra and underwear while Dana Kaufmann picked tiny insects off her body. She was like a mother gorilla grooming her offspring, hands moving swiftly and expertly over every patch of Susan's skin. Cast skins covered Susan's body, crusted on like patches of eczema. Her torso was smeared with brown feces. Dana found three bugs still biting, latched in a neat row on Susan's lower stomach, just above her waistline. The exterminator pulled them free one by one—muttering, "Sorry," each time Susan winced at the tug of the bug's unlatching.

"Hold still."

Kaufmann reached between Susan's legs and plucked an insect from just below the crotch, where it was about to bite. "Excuse my reach," she grunted.

Susan nodded blankly. "What time is it?"

She felt completely disoriented: her back ached terribly, and her head was pounding like she'd been hit with a shovel. And, Jesus Christ, the itching—her whole body itched, one massive undifferentiated fiery itch.

"Quarter to ten. Here." Kaufmann produced a tube of calamine lotion from a pocket of her coveralls and handed it to Susan as she continued. "I was supposed to be here yesterday, and I apologize. I had an emergency call at a house in Ditmas, and frankly you were not a priority, since I had already cleared the premises."

Kaufmann paused, shaking her head in disgust and self-recrimination. "I cannot imagine how I failed to detect a problem of this magnitude. I honestly do not know how it happened. I just didn't see them."

Susan closed her eyes against the sun, which was shining in brutally through the kitchen windows. "They didn't want you to see them."

Kaufmann cocked her head. "Who didn't want me to see them?"

"They were hiding from you. Only I was supposed to see them. Only me." Tears were rolling from her eyes, down her red and abraded cheeks.

"Stop. Susan, hold on."

"They're not . . . " Susan's voice dropped to a whisper, and she looked around fearfully. The bugs, emboldened by their assault on her the night before, roamed at will across the floor of the kitchen, in fat roving packs. *This is their house now.* "They're not normal. They're . . . they're supernatural. I read this book, see . . . "

"Don't tell me." Kaufmann scowled with irritation. "*The Shadow Species.*"

"You've heard of it?"

"I wish I could say I hadn't. All right. You're clean." Kaufmann cracked her knuckles, jerked a thumb at the pile of clothes in the corner of the room. "But I would not advise putting those back on."

So Susan wrapped herself in Kaufmann's Greater Brooklyn Pest Control jacket while the exterminator heaped scorn upon Pullman Thibodaux's masterpiece. "Badbugs, right? Please. Just for starters, the author of that book was insane. Literally. A mental patient. Supposedly, he and his wife had a severe bedbug infestation, and he was too cheap to have it treated professionally. So he's trying to handle it, doing all this research, taping up the mattresses, all the bullshit things people do when they don't know what they're doing."

Susan listened, holding her breath.

"Long story short, the wife can't take it anymore, she walks. The guy goes cuckoo for Cocoa Puffs, decides that bedbugs aren't bed-bugs, they're demons. OK?" Kaufmann, without smiling, rotated one finger beside her temple, playground sign language for crazy. "So he wrote that book"—she placed exaggerated air quotes around the word—"in his spare time, while in the nuthouse."

"Well . . . all right, but . . . "

"Susan, I had a client a couple years ago who got his hands on that damn book and insisted to me that his house had been cursed. Except he didn't say curse, he said . . . oh, what the hell did he say?"

"Blight," mumbled Susan. A draft crept in beneath the frame of the kitchen window, and she shivered. She was starting to feel a little ridiculous, half-naked and wrapped in Kaufmann's gigantic jacket.

"Yes. Blight. Well, I performed an aggressive three-pronged protocol, right out of the playbook, and guess what? Five years later, he's contented and bedbug free."

The words shone like a dawning ray of hope in Susan's mind: *contented and bedbug free*. But still . . . she cleared her throat, shook her head. "But . . . " Susan gestured around the apartment. "There are so many of them."

"I've seen worse." Kaufmann looked around. "Well, not worse. But close."

"But I couldn't *kill* them. They can't be *killed*."

"Oh, yeah?"

In a swift, athletic motion, Dana Kaufmann squatted and snatched a bedbug between two thick fingers. A split second later, she held up the squashed corpse for Susan's inspection: a crumbled brown shell, a tiny gush of bright red blood at its center.

"Dead."

Susan reached forward with a trembling hand and wiped the bug's bloody broken body off Kaufmann's fingertip onto her own. "Jesus," she whispered. She began to shake, overcome by a confusing wash of shame and fear. "Dana. Dana, I tried to murder my husband last night. With a butcher's knife."

The exterminator raised her eyebrows slightly, let out a long low whistle, and shrugged. "Well, you know, infestations place extraordinary strain upon a relationship."

Despite everything, Susan laughed.

"Now, come on," said Kaufmann. "Let's kill some fucking bedbugs."

*

"The first thing we do is, we clean. Here, and your landlady's apartment. Basement, too. This entire building needs to be scoured, disinfected, and decluttered, down to the canvas. No hiding places: no bugs."

"But the book . . . "

"Right, right. The book. Your friend the mental patient wrote that the curse of the evil bedbugs will stay with you forever and always, no matter what you do or where you go. Well, guess what? The ancient Greeks said if you baked the bedbugs in a pie with meat and beans, they'd cure malaria. That, too, was total nonsense."

Susan smiled weakly.

"Here's what is *not* nonsense. We're going to vacuum every room, we're going to steam clean your mattresses and linens, we're going to dry clean every piece of fabric in this apartment. We're going to scour every exposed surface. Then we pack up your infestibles to be sealed and pumped with Vikane."

"Vikane?"

"A fumigant. Industrial strength. Forty-eight hours in Vikane, no bug lives. No egg lives. Nothing. Then we proceed to the application of silica gel and pyrethroids." Dana Kaufmann's confidence, her sense of power and purpose, was palpable. She was like a general, rallying for battle. "Do you have a vacuum cleaner with a hose attachment?"

"In the closet."

"Good. You relax. Drink your coffee."

Susan did as she was told, slowly sipping from her mug and taking deep, cleansing breaths, watching the sunbeams play across the handsome brown hardwood of the kitchen floor. Already it seemed like there were fewer bedbugs than there had been an hour ago, when Kaufmann first pulled her from the bonus room. She heard the vacuum cleaner roar to life and allowed herself to hope that maybe Kaufmann was right: she would clean, they would pack her infestibles in Vikane, apply the pyrethroids and the silica dust and whatever else . . . and, in time, everything would be OK. Everything would go back to—

"Oh, shit," Susan said suddenly. "Alex. I have really got to call Alex."

She had recovered her iPhone in the morning, found it in a corner of the bonus room, shut off with a dozen bedbugs nesting in the UBS slot at the base. Now she turned it on, but before she could dial her husband, it rang. The incoming number was one she didn't recognize, a 718 area code.

"Hello?"

"Hi, this is . . . "

The mechanical roar of the vacuum was moving down the hallway now, coming closer.

"What?"

"I'm—"

"Hold on."

Susan lowered the phone and shouted to the living room. "Dana, can you cut the vacuum for one second?" Susan turned back to the phone. She had to call her husband. He must be worried sick.

Except—he was supposed to come back, come back to get her. Where was Alex?

"I'm sorry . . . who is this?"

"My name is Jack Barnum. I think I used to live in your apartment."

A nervous, prickly energy erupted into Susan's chest. Beneath thick smears of calamine lotion, her itches sang to life. Kaufmann poked her head into the kitchen, holding up the vacuum hose with an inquiring expression. "Can I . . . ?" Susan shook her head "no," and the exterminator set it down with a sour expression.

"Yes, Jack? Yes, you did." She held the phone with her chin, reached around to scratch beneath her shoulder blades.

"I read the note you sent to Jessie, on Facebook. I finally figured out her password. It was my middle name. That was her password, my middle name . . . my . . . " Susan could hear raw, throaty grief in his voice, grief and bafflement.

Alarm bells were clanging in Susan's mind. She scratched the sole of her right foot with the craggy big toenail of her left. "Jack? Are you there?"

"Yeah. Yeah, I am. Do you know where she is? Did you—Jesus, did you find her?"

"No, I'm sorry. I don't know where she is. Jack, can you tell me what happened in this apartment?"

Jack Barnum said nothing, but she heard his agonized, fearful breathing, tearful and labored. Dana Kaufmann, not one to waste a spare moment, was now crouched on all fours beneath the kitchen sink, right at Susan's feet, scouring the baseboards with a thick-bristled brush.

"What happened, Jack?"

"She . . . Jessie . . . poor Jessie, she got this idea, somehow. That we had bedbugs. And I didn't believe her. Because I never saw them. Never. And she . . . " His voice trembled again, and petered out. "She . . . "

"She tried to kill you."

"Yes. Jesus, how did you know that?"

Oh, God—oh, God—they were already here. The bugs were here before Jessie and Jack even moved in. Shivers chased up and down Susan's spine like electric pulses. Her whole body itched: searing, dry, tingling, horrible itches. *They were already here.*

"Anyway, so, I freaked out, and I mean, I just ran." Jack sobbed again, a single guttural wail. "I left her here."

Dana was watching Susan now, looking up at her with her head tilted and one eyebrow raised.

"And then they kept torturing her," Susan said. "And she flipped out, and, and when she couldn't take it anymore, she bolted. She left so fast she left the cat behind. And—"

"The cat?"

"What?"

A cheery knock sounded at the front door. "Yoo-hoo?" called the genial, throaty voice. "Suze?"

"No," Jack said. "We never had a cat."

Dana was on her feet and out of the kitchen, halfway down the hall, while Susan stared into dead air, thoughts tumbling into her brain:

Never had a cat.

The knock came again, a happy little "shave-and-a-haircut" knock.

"Wait, Dana! Don't—"

It was too late. The exterminator pulled the door open and Andrea Scharfstein smashed the side of her head with a hammer. Kaufmann stepped back, swayed on her feet and pivoted toward Susan, an expression of dumb surprise frozen on her face. Then she pivoted again, back toward Andrea, and Susan saw the inside of her head where her forehead had been cracked like a pumpkin, clumps of red and gray under the cap of her skull. Andrea twirled the hammer in her hand and struck again, this time with the claw side, tearing a huge, messy divot into Kaufman's face. While her hand, still clutching the hammer, hovered in the space between them, a badbug flitted from the open cut on Andrea's arm into the shattered wreck of Dana's face, like a child cannonballing into a swimming pool.

Dana's broken frame sunk to the floor, and Andrea Scharfstein looked up at Susan with a daffy grin. "Oh, dear," she said, clucking. "What a shame, what a shame."

The bugs appeared from everywhere at once: they poured from the loose electrical outlet; they swarmed up out of the floorboards; vomited up from the sink. Susan raced for the knife block and slipped on the fallen ceiling tile, still lying at an odd angle in the center of the kitchen floor. Her foot danced out from under her and she landed with a painful, spine-rattling thud, sunny-side up on the kitchen floor. Spots flickered before her eyes while badbugs advanced from all directions.

Andrea was coming, too, padding toward Susan in her god-awful lime green house shoes, step by step. The bugs crawled up and down Susan's arms in exultant figure eights. Susan felt them in her hair.

*

Though Susan's body was weak and frail, it nevertheless took Andrea a full half hour to drag her down the long hallway into the living room, and then across the room to the air shaft. At last she made it and then, with a slippered heel, managed to kick open one of the windows lining the shaft. Cold air whistled into the room, and a moment later Susan heard the distant crash of glass hitting the basement floor.

"Now, listen, dear," Andrea said, bending over Susan. "This is going to hurt. And there will definitely be some blood. Actually, if I'm being totally honest, there will be a lot of blood." Andrea grimaced apologetically, her thin tight face a map of lines and spots. "But the thing is, dear, that's how they want you."

Andrea lifted her just far enough to get her up and over the sill and shoved her into the air shaft. As she tumbled down two floors to the basement, Susan imagined herself as a baby carriage, spinning end over end, filled with blood, about to burst on the floor below.

29.

The pain was terrible. It radiated upward from the lower part of her body, from her legs and her pelvis.

Susan could not actually *see* the lower part of her body. Or anything, really. She was propped upright, somehow, and could move her head around a little, but not enough to look down. And anyway, it was dark. Terribly dark. But she could *feel* it, that was for certain. She could feel the pain, searing and intense, wave upon wave of agonizing pain radiating up from her legs. They were broken, she was sure of that. She tried, tentatively, to move them, and the waves of pain doubled, crested. Her right kneecap was facing the wrong way, is what it felt like. Her left leg she could not feel at all.

Next Susan became aware of the stench. Wherever she was—*the trunk of a car? stuffed upright in a hole somewhere?*—it smelled *awful*. The smell filled her nose and mouth, stung her eyes with tears. It was like the hot rancid odor that trails after trash trucks, that lifts from the muggy city streets on scorching August mornings: a reek of garbage and shit and death and decay. The smell was all around her. She was inside it.

She could move her shoulder and her arms. The joints were stiff and resistant, but they moved. She wiggled her fingers and they moved through something, something loose and slippery, crumbling.

Garbage—she was buried in garbage. She pushed her fingers around her, expanding the radius of discovery: soil and dirt. Hunks of slimy, roughly textured vegetable matter, slippery shreds and waxy peels, crumbling wet hunks of what felt like cardboard.

Oh, Susan thought simply. *I'm in the compost bin.*

She extended her fingertips as far as they would go, swimming them through the clustered muck, and they brushed against walls of hard plastic. She reached up, wincing as the joints in her shoulders cracked, and touched the lid of the bin above her head. She was able to raise the lid the tiniest bit before it fell closed again.

Slowly, she lowered her hands again, and they brushed against flesh. Susan screamed. As she screamed, Susan stared forward, and her eyes had adjusted to the darkness enough to see that Jessica Spender was staring back at her, her eyes wide open, bugs crawling across the milky flesh of the eyeballs.

Susan screamed and screamed and screamed, the stench of rotting trash filling her mouth and rolling like fog down into her lungs.

*

In time, Susan stopped screaming, lapsed into a low animal moan, and then into terrified silence.

The minutes rolled past.

There was nothing to do, nothing to think. She couldn't move. She kept her eyes closed, rather than stare into the dead eyes of Jessica Spender. But with her eyes closed, she imagined the body of Dana Kaufmann, slowly being covered over with gleeful triumphant bugs, her blood leaching onto the kitchen floor, a bloodsucker's feast.

Susan flickered in and out of consciousness, her head lolling forward on occasion, then jerking back up when her mouth sank below the line of the garbage. The pain, which had been so sharp when she woke, dampened to a low constant ache. In time, Susan began to feel a strange fondness for this pain, radiating up from the wreckage of her legs: it distracted her from the itching, rashy sensation that had been her constant preoccupation for so long. It was a different kind of pain, and for that she felt a perverse gratitude.

She waited, not knowing what she was waiting for. Andrea had stuffed her in here and gone somewhere—but would she be coming back? One thing she knew was that Dana Kaufmann, poor, dead Dana, had been very wrong. So had Alex, and so had stupid Dr. Lucas Gerstein. Pullman Thibodaux was right, lunatic or not. The badbugs were real, though they had come to 56 Cranberry Street long ago . . . before Susan and Alex, before Jessica and Jack.

Susan eyes slipped closed. She didn't care. She wanted to die.

Except for Emma. Oh, my dear little darling girl, Susan thought, and slipped away again.

*

Susan did not die.

Sometime later—there was no time in here, no sense of time, only dull pain and stretches of sort-of sleep, and the smell—Susan heard the door. Heavy wood dragging against unfinished concrete with a dismal, echoing scrape. The strange small door that led from beneath the stoop into the basement. Susan's heart began to pound. *Let it be anyone,* she thought. *Anyone but her.*

"Please . . ." Susan croaked, her voice thin and broken, the metal scritch of a broken spring. "Please, help."

The lid of the compost bin yawned open, and Andrea's wrinkled old face, with the cat's-eye glasses balanced on the end of her nose, hovered into view above Susan's eye line, like a horrid bizarro-world sun rising on the horizon. Andrea made kind of a *tsk-tsk* noise, a parent disappointed at her daughter's dirty dorm room.

"I didn't mean for any of this to happen," Andrea began abruptly, "So don't go around blaming me."

"Andrea," Susan managed. "Andrea, please."

Still holding up the lid with one hand, Andrea removed her glasses with the other, and Susan saw in her eyes that steely faraway look, the one she'd seen last night . . . or was it last week? Whenever Andrea had come for help with her phone. *Except that's not why she came. She came to make sure you didn't leave. To remind you of the hotel. To make sure you drove Alex away, to get you alone—*

"Andrea, please."

"If you must blame someone, blame Howard. Forty-six years we were married!"

"Please. My daughter, Andrea."

"Forty-six years!"

Andrea propped the lid open with a hunk of two-by-four and walked away, her face disappearing from Susan's view. But she kept talking, the sound of her voice now drifting to Susan from the far side of the room.

"Can you imagine how it felt to be told, after all those years, that he is not in love with you anymore? That he is now in love with your neighbor? With stupid Norma Frohm? That he has been making love with her, every Saturday afternoon he has been making love with her, while you are at the grocery store, for seventeen years?"

It came again, as it had last night, a scrap of text dancing up in

Susan's feverish mind:

Someone has to commit the act, think the thought that throws open the door to the darkness.

It wasn't Alex, of course. And it wasn't poor Jack Barnum, either.

Andrea kept talking, her voice still coming from the other side of the room, now competing with the noise of a drawer opening, the sound of Andrea rummaging, looking for something. Susan's left leg throbbed, sending desperate distress calls up her spinal cord to the base of her brain.

"Oh, Suze, I was so angry. I was just so terribly angry." She had returned to the bin now, her wraith's head back where Susan could see it. "I just . . . I wanted him to suffer. I did. Oh, how I prayed to God that he would suffer."

"Andrea," Susan said again. "Andrea."

The old lady shook her head rapidly, grinning her lunatic vaudeville grin. "And then, just like that: He did! He suffered! The bugs came, and he suffered so terribly. God, you should have seen how he suffered. *And I laughed.*" Andrea laughed now, low and throaty and maniacal. Susan shuddered in the darkness.

"Please, Andrea. Please . . . my daughter . . . "

"I laughed because I was so happy," Andrea said and then dropped into a confidential whisper. "God had answered my prayers."

She held up a small jar, like the kind used to can preserves. Susan couldn't see what was inside.

"But you know, Susan, I'm going to be totally honest with you. I don't think it was God that sent them. I don't think it was God at all."

In one swift, efficient motion, Andrea twisted the lid off the jar and overturned it into the compost bin, shaking it up and down over

Susan's head like a saltshaker. The bugs rained down into her hair, onto her shoulders, into her eyes, and when Susan opened her mouth to scream they landed like snowflakes on her tongue.

"So, you see, it's not my fault." Andrea's voice was pleading, pitiful, even as she kept pouring in the bugs, and Susan kept screaming, writhing helplessly in the darkness, while the bugs begin to bite into her face, her neck, her arms, her shoulders. "They run the show now. It's not my fault."

"So kill me," Susan spat with effort, her tongue crawling with bugs. "Let them have me."

"Oh no, oh no," Andrea said. "You don't understand. They need you alive." She dropped the lid and Susan heard her, walking away. "As long as you last, anyway."

*

The badbugs bit unceasingly, scaling Susan's body, climbing happily in and out of the rises and folds of her flesh, latching themselves on, biting her over and over. Occasionally, Susan would reach up desperately, knowing it was useless, trying to maneuver her hands up far enough to throw open the lid of the bin. But it was impossible, and each effort sent new waves of pain radiating down her spine.

She gave up, and the badbugs continued their eager efforts. After an hour, they began to subside; she felt them dropping off, scuttling away into the infinite hiding places afforded by the compost bin, to sleep and digest their meals. But they would wake and feed again— she knew that. And how many more jars did Andrea have . . .

She breathed deeply through her mouth, in and out, forcing herself to think. *I have to convince her to let me go.* There is a person in there still, somewhere, deep down was the person that once was Andrea Scharfstein, before this blight took hold of her.

Somehow, I have to get through to her.

Susan had been trying not to look at Jessica Spender, her head tilted at a terrible unnatural angle, her tongue lolling out of her mouth. In the breast pocket of her shirt, Susan noticed for the first time, was a severed finger. She blinked and looked closer. It was a girl's finger, slim and manicured, with an engagement ring on it.

Jessica's own finger, surely.

Ping.

Ping.

Jessica had managed, somehow, to open the bin, to get her hand out far enough to tap on the glass of the air shaft. She had sent a desperate noise, the metallic ping of a gold band rapping on glass: an SOS, echoing up the air shaft.

And I had told Andrea about it, and she had cut off her finger.

There would be no convincing Andrea Scharfstein of anything. For her to be freed of this horror, either she would have to die, or Andrea would.

*

The badbugs began to bite again, as Susan had known they would. Suddenly, there were dozens of the tiny monsters feasting on her, finding fresh patches, new stretches of flesh that hadn't yet been pierced. Some stayed latched on; some ate quickly and then dropped away, replaced by a fresh attacker or leaving behind a new itch, an itch that couldn't be scratched.

Susan shouted with renewed desperation and again reached her arms upward, straining her muscles as far as they could go, managing to push the lid only very slightly farther than she had before, before she had to let go and it fell closed again. "Damn it," Susan cried, tears flooding her eyes. She tossed her whole body with frustration, moving the tiniest bit—a quarter of an inch, maybe—to one side, and then back. The bin rattled a little, and she felt it move around her.

"Huh," Susan said.

She shook her body again, on purpose this time, and again felt the bin rattle. She did it again, shaking herself as hard as she could, leaning forward, wriggling back, and feeling the bin move under her weight. With desperate force, she heaved herself forward, and the bin heaved forward, too.

She stopped, took a breath, and then heaved herself backward. The bin heaved backward.

Holy shit, she thought. *It's working.*

She heaved forward and back again, and the compost rustled and shifted all around her.

She did it a third time, the bin jerked, and Jessica Spender's corpse slipped in the garbage and soil, the dead face resettling into a new patch of muck.

Susan kept it up, pushing harder and harder, until at last the whole can pitched forward, spilling her and Jessica out, out into a sliding pile of shit and dirt and eggshells and coffee grounds, out onto the cement floor of the basement. Susan screamed in triumph, her heart pounding, even as her entire body flared with pain. She tried to stand and collapsed, her legs broken and useless beneath her. Breathing deeply, Susan heaved herself up onto her arms and looked around wildly for the door.

She dragged herself forward, inch by painful inch, moaning with the effort, her chafed sandpaper skin rubbing raw against the cold concrete. Behind the overturned compost bin, past a second bin still standing upright beside the first one, past a row of milk crates full of tools and cleansers. Painted on one dingy wall like a gruesome mural was a sloppy circle of blackish red, an ancient grisly stain, the ghostly remains of Howard's violent escape. Halfway to the door was an old trunk, black and battered. Susan grabbed onto the back of it and used it to heave herself forward—and then stopped abruptly, resting her head on the dented top of the trunk, breathing heavily. She moved her fingers and worked at the latch.

Susan heard the squeak and scrape behind her as the basement door swung open. She jerked her head around, spots like dancing fireworks before her eyes, and glimpsed a rectangle of daylight behind Andrea before the old lady, grinning like a death's head in her cat's-eye sunglasses, pulled the door closed behind her.

"Oh, goodness," crowed Andrea. "Look who's out of bed."

From one of her frail old hands dangled the claw hammer, bits of Dana Kaufmann's blood and brain still clinging to the claw.

"I can't let you go, Suze." Andrea advanced across the cold floor of the basement. The one dim lightbulb swung gently between them. "We *need* you."

Susan grunted, slammed shut the door of the trunk, and angled her body up toward Andrea.

"What—what is that?" said Andrea. She dropped the hammer, raised her hands to her mouth, trembling. "Where did you find that?"

Susan had found it in the trunk, just where Louis had told her it would be. She raised it, propping her elbows on the top of the trunk, aimed the long nose of the old rifle's barrel at Andrea's torso, and pulled the trigger.

Epilogue

It was the gunshot, Alex later explained, that brought him rushing down the stairs and into the basement. At first he thought the shot came from somewhere inside the apartment, so loud and nearby had it sounded. But then he realized it had come booming up from the basement, amplified and distorted by the airshaft. When the shot sounded, he had been standing in the doorway of the apartment, contemplating the corpse of Dana Kaufmann, which in a span of five hours had been entirely consumed; a handful of bugs was crawling in and out of the empty eye sockets, picking at what flesh remained.

In the basement Alex discovered the two of them, collapsed a few feet from each other: Andrea's dead body and Susan's, barely living. Alex lifted his wife close to his chest, ignoring the bugs that were swarming over her body, and carried her toward daylight and safety.

"I'm sorry," he murmured over and over, though Susan was unconscious, her pulse barely registering in her neck. "I'm so sorry."

He said it again when she woke in the hospital, said, "I'm sorry," and hugged her so tightly that the nurse said, "Easy, buddy," and gently separated them.

"You're sorry?" whispered Susan. "I tried to kill you."

"Yeah, well." Alex stroked her hand and smiled. "You were un-successful. That makes a world of difference."

Emma was at Alex's parents' house, in Roslyn Harbor. She was fine, and missed her mommy.

"I want to see her."

"When you're up and about. . . . "

"I want to see her."

Alex nodded. "Of course. Now you need to rest, OK? When I come back, I'll bring her. She's going to be so excited."

Susan leaned back into the pile of pillows, looked dreamily around at the gleaming whiteness of the hospital room, the row of machines, the drips feeding various fluids into her arms, feeling no pain—and, she realized with a warm gush of relief, feeling no itches.

Her eyes were half closed and Alex was at the door, slowly pulling it closed, when her eyes shot open. The dream—the hammers—

"What about Louis?"

*

The crime-scene investigators had found Louis King in the second compost bin, his head protruding like a puppet's from where he'd been buried neck deep in garbage, just as Susan had been, and Jessica before her. His forehead bore a deep indentation, at dead center; the hammer blow had driven the front part of his skull deep into his brain. The newspaper quoted one policeman as reporting that bedbugs were swarming over his forehead and cheeks, more bedbugs were crawling over his eyes.

When those same detectives turned up in the hospital to interview Susan about what happened, they used that same word—"bedbugs," with an "e"—and she made no effort to correct them.

*

"So," said Susan Wendt, on the night of February 12, as she and
Alex shared a bottle of wine in the living room of their new 2,050-
square-foot home in Montclair, New Jersey. "Theresa?"

Alex looked at her blankly for a moment and then burst out
laughing. "Hey, what can I say? It was the most realistic name I could
think of, with a knife to my throat."

"What knife? Who had a knife?"

"Nothing, boo-boo."

Emma had come prancing down the stairs, naked except for her
rain boots and a pair of pink fairy wings. "Is anybody going to give
me a bath? Fairies need baths!"

Alex had declared himself on vacation through the winter, turning over GemFlex to Vic, while Susan, on doctor's orders, was doing
pretty much nothing until her legs and skin were healed. They'd been
visiting preschools as a family and zeroed in on a place called New
Jersey Families, which Alex loved because it sounded like a Mafia-run
preschool. Susan thought it was clean, bright, and charming, and
Emma deemed the lead teacher, Ms. Jessica, "pretty much amazing,
pretty much."

They new house had a decent-sized yard, so they'd gotten a mutt
from the North Shore Animal League, a good-natured squirmy
puppy that Susan named Kaufmann.

*

Every night, before going to sleep, Susan Wendt stood naked before the mirror in her leg casts, examining her body carefully, tracking the progress of her healing. Her many scars were already fading, the welts receding from angry red to pale pink, then away to nothing, as welts are supposed to do. Some nights, when she performed this ritual, studying her flesh inch by inch, Susan allowed herself to believe that it might be over. If *The Shadow Species* had it right—and so far, unfortunately, it had been right in every detail—then the blight had been lifted with Andrea's death.

Some nights she believed it, and some nights she didn't. Every morning, when she woke, she lay in bed for a long time, until she felt ready to check her pillowcase.

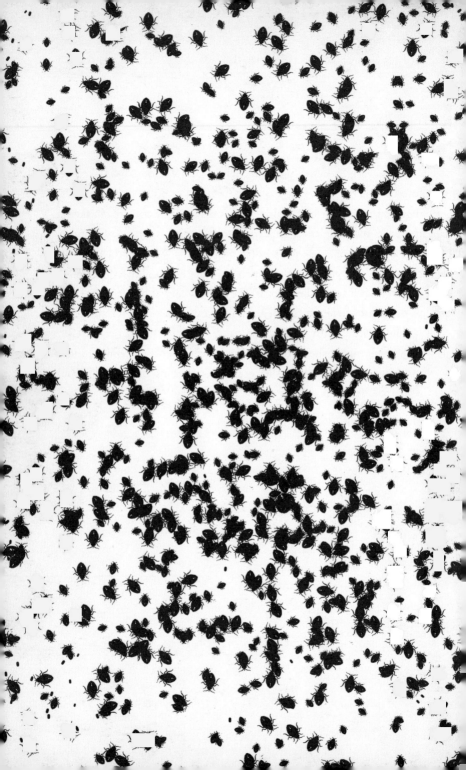

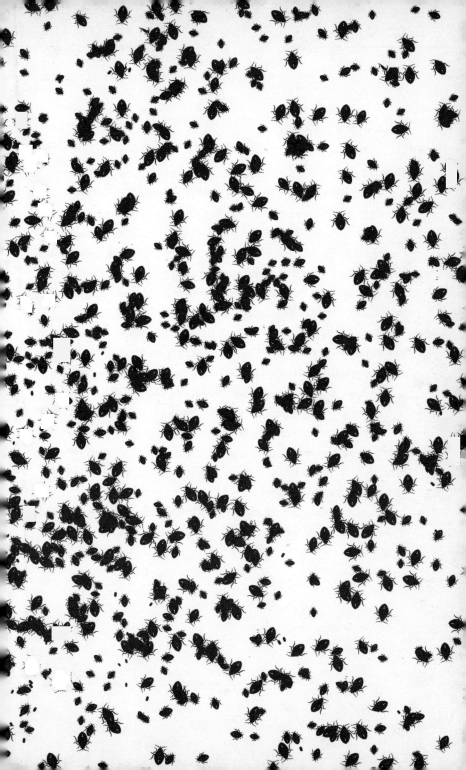

Special Thanks

To Kate Samworth for teaching me about oil painting, and especially for presenting me with the verb to *scumble*. Kate's remarkable paintings, which are neither supernatural nor evil, can be found at KateSamworth.com Thanks to my friend Ed Parrinello, of SquareMoose Photography in Manhattan, for the basics of high-end jewelry and watch photography. And many, many thanks to James at Flash Exterminating in Brooklyn, who was generous with his time during what has become an unending busy season for the industry.

A tip of the hat to the habitués of Bedbugger.com, where I have lurked, bedbuglike, for many hours, gathering insights and then disappearing, sated, into the darkness. What a great and terrifying website.

Thanks, as always, to my fantastic agent, Molly Lyons.

Thanks to Jason Rekulak at Quirk Books, who continues to lead me, Virgil-like, down new paths of adventure. I am fortunate beyond words to be working once again with him as well as with Doogie, Melissa, Eric, Mary Ellen, Robin, Stephen, Dave, Brett—all you lunatics. Thanks, Quirk Books.

Last, and most, thanks to Diana Winters, who told me I should write this book, helped me write it, and made it better when she read it.